O9-ABF-292

HANG OUT THE FLAG

★ ★ ★ ★ ★ ★ ★

HANG OUT THE FLAG

★ ★ ★ ★ ★ ★ ★

Katherine McGlade Marko

Macmillan Publishing Company   New York

Maxwell Macmillan Canada   Toronto

Maxwell Macmillan International
New York   Oxford   Singapore   Sydney

The author wishes to extend a note of thanks to the staff of the Gail Borden Public Library in Elgin, Illinois, for all the assistance they so kindly rendered.

Macmillan Publishing Company is part of the
Maxwell Communication Group of Companies.

Macmillan Publishing Company
866 Third Avenue, New York, NY 10022

Maxwell Macmillan Canada, Inc.
1200 Eglinton Avenue East, Suite 200
Don Mills, Ontario M3C 3N1

First edition
Printed in the United States of America

10 9 8 7 6 5 4 3 2 1

The text of this book is set in 12 point Sabon.

Library of Congress Cataloging-in-Publication Data
Marko, Katherine.
Hang out the flag / Katherine McGlade Marko. — 1st ed.
     p.   cm.
   Summary: In 1943, as she waits for her father to come home on leave, a sixth-grade girl in a midwestern town tries to find something special to do for the war effort.
ISBN 0-02-762320-3
1. World War, 1939–1945—United States—Juvenile fiction.
[1. World War, 1939–1945—United States—Fiction. 2. Family life—Fiction. 3. Schools—Fiction. 4. Spies—Fiction.] I. Title.
PZ7.M3397Han 1992   [Fic]—dc20   92-349

To my husband, Alex,
who served with the Fifth Army Air Corps in the
South Pacific during World War II

AUTHOR'S NOTE

The United States was plunged into World War II on December 7, 1941, with the sneak attack by the Japanese on Pearl Harbor in Hawaii. Four days later, Germany declared war on the United States. Soon after, American troops were fighting in Europe, Asia, Africa, and islands of the South Pacific. American men and high school boys joined the armed forces so fast it was difficult to keep track of friends and relatives. Thousands of others were drafted.

Among the first servicemen to enter a war zone were members of the Seabees—the construction battalion of the United States Navy. The Seabees built roads, airfields, and bases and maintained them.

American women joined the work force in record numbers. All Americans, even children, recycled everything that would help the war effort. Patriotism was high.

The war had been raging for almost two years when this story begins. It is a story of the home front in a midwestern town.

1

As Leslie Jamieson came down the stairs, she yawned sleepily and muttered, "I didn't think sixth grade would be so tough." She wished she could have solved her arithmetic problems the night before. Then she wouldn't have had to get up early.

She heard the radio in the kitchen. Her mother listened to all the news programs—but at this time of the morning? Usually Mama had left for work by now. The commentator was giving the latest reports from the battlefronts.

Leslie flopped into a chair at the kitchen table. "War!" She was sick of it. But what could she expect in September 1943? She thought of her father and felt guilty for griping. Papa was in the Seabees.

Pushing her long hair behind her ears, Leslie yawned again. "Morning, Mama." She glanced at the radio. "Gee, I'd hate to live in those bombed-out countries."

"Yes, dear." Mama flicked off the radio. "So would I."

The lines on Mama's forehead deepened. Leslie knew why—any day Papa could leave boot camp for a far-off place like Europe or the South Pacific.

Again, Leslie felt guilty. Oh, she did her part for the war effort, collecting newspapers, tin cans, and grease. But all the kids did that. If she were grown up, she would be a war correspondent, since she wanted to be a writer someday. Right now, though, she had to go to school, do chores, and keep an eye on her brother, eight-year-old Kenny. How she envied her cousin Ruthie, who lived with her mother up the street. Ruthie was seventeen and worked in a munitions plant.

By now, Leslie thought, she was even ready to listen to Buddy Haver. She had overheard Buddy say yesterday, after school, that he knew of a Nazi spy living right there in Emmetsville. To be in on catching an enemy would really be something grand—something that surely would make Papa proud of her.

Leslie always felt left out when Papa praised Ruthie, who was at their house so often that she almost lived with them. If only once she could do something better than Ruthie.

But with Buddy Haver! He was always bragging. None of the kids believed him, and he fell over his own feet so often that they didn't even want to play with him. Sometimes, coming home from school, he hung on to her and her best friend, Mary DeJohn. That always riled her.

But yesterday, when he was telling the boys about the Nazi, Leslie thought he'd mentioned the name Oscar. The only Oscar she knew was Mr. Von Desch, who lived at the end of Laramie—her street, where it stopped at First Avenue. Still, she guessed, Buddy was probably just bragging again.

"Why are you up so early?" Mama cut in on her thoughts.

"I have to finish my homework." As she reached for her books, which were lying on the chair where she had left them, she glanced at the wall clock. "Aren't you late for work?" Mama was supposed to be at the Overton Steel office at seven-thirty. And she had to take the trolley to the southeastern edge of town. Like many other steel plants, Overton was committed to making war materials for the duration.

"Yes, I forgot to set the alarm." Mama drained her coffee cup and stood up. She was a tall woman, but her shoulders slumped. Leslie twisted a strand of her hair. She wished Mama didn't have to work.

Soon she heard the slap-slap of Kenny's slippers in the hallway. "It's early," he grumbled as he joined her and Mama.

Mama laughed and touseled his light hair, so like her own. Leslie often wished she looked like Mama, too, but she had Papa's stiff dark hair and green, brown-speckled eyes.

Leslie missed Papa and hoped the war would be over before he could be sent somewhere like those "war-torn" places the commentator spoke about. Well, she was going to do something special when he came home on leave—whenever that was. Ruthie was knitting him a sweater and was always running in to show Mama her progress with it. "I'd sure love to do something to make that sweater look dumb," Leslie told herself, but so far she could think of nothing outstanding.

Mama bustled about as she prepared to leave. "You will both get on with your breakfast now," she said, gesturing toward the box of cornflakes and the bottle of milk on the table. She smoothed her gray suit and added, "It's almost time for the trolley."

"Why don't you take a taxi?" Kenny asked. "Ruthie does when she's late."

"It's too expensive for me," Mama answered. "Ruthie doesn't have to keep a house and family going."

Leslie snorted at her cousin's name. The thing about Ruthie that bothered her most was Ruthie's feelings for Papa. Ruthie's father had died when she was little, and ever since she'd acted as if Papa were her father as much as Leslie's and Kenny's. And Papa had always exclaimed over her gifts and good marks when she was in school and patted her shoulder whenever she was discouraged. He was her mother's first cousin. Leslie twisted a strand of her hair again. She guessed she was jealous, but who wouldn't be?

Leslie was jolted by the sound of the doorbell.

"Who could that be at this time of day?" Mama said as she went to answer it.

Leslie followed her and peeked out the front window. "It's the florist's truck."

She heard the driver ask, "Mrs. Jamieson?"

"Yes." Mama signed the slip. "You sure are early."

"Have to be, Ma'am. Our other driver was drafted into the army. Bye, now."

Mama opened the long box. In it lay a dozen beautiful yellow roses. Leaning over to smell their fragrance, she murmured, "Oh, my favorite." Then she set the box on the table and snatched up the card. "They're from Papa. Today's our anniversary." Her eyes, amber like Kenny's, beamed.

Leslie was surprised. "You didn't say anything."

"I guess I didn't want to think of it too much with Papa away. But he's coming home. Oh, I'm so happy." Mama ended with a little squeal in her voice. She held the card tightly in both hands.

Excitement flooded Leslie. "Papa's coming home? I can't wait!" She'd have to really get busy now if she was going to have something special ready for him.

"Yippee!" Kenny shouted. "We can play pitch and catch. When?"

Mama glanced at the card. "In two and one-half weeks."

Kenny's smile disappeared. "I thought it might be tomorrow. Nobody can pitch as good as Papa." Kenny always said he wanted to be a ballplayer when he grew up—like Babe Ruth. "I'm going to practice like mad till Papa gets here."

Mama picked up the box and buried her face in the roses. "Please put them in the blue vase after I leave, Leslie."

Leslie nodded. Mama patted the back of her up-swept hairdo. "And now," she went on, "I will need some new stockings. After school, you will go to Benjamin's and get me a pair of nylons if you can."

If is right, Leslie thought. Most of the nylon made now was used for parachutes for the Air Corps, so nylon stockings were awfully scarce. But this was Tuesday, and Benjamin's usually received their hosiery orders on Tuesday, the saleslady had told Mama. Mama was never able to make it. By the time she reached the store after work, it was almost five o'clock, and they were all sold out. Leslie could be there by three-thirty.

"Okay, Mama."

"If there aren't any nylons, they may have some rayons."

Well, rayon was nice, too, Leslie thought, but nylon was nicer. It dried more quickly, too.

"And," Mama continued, "you will tell the clerk to charge them."

Mama always said "you will" when she gave an order. Papa always said, "Will you *please*," but the *please* came out stronger than the other words, so Leslie recognized his orders as easily as she did Mama's.

Leslie was glad they didn't need ration coupons for stockings, as they did for sugar or meat or shoes. Those little books of coupons, issued to everyone, were a pain. But so much was needed for the armed forces, the coupons were necessary to give civilians a fair share of what was left.

Mama kept talking as she headed for the front door. "Now I must hurry or I'll miss the trolley. Leslie, watch out for Kenny, and, Kenny, you will listen to your sister."

Leslie hated when Mama said that. It sounded as though all she was good for was doing chores and keeping an eye on Kenny.

But Mama had a new spring in her step and Leslie knew it was because of Papa's flowers. She thought of Papa now, with his ready grin that could disappear as fast as it came. Sometimes it looked as if Papa swallowed his smile before he was through smiling. He was tall and thin and his face always looked tanned. He should have been a teacher or scientist, Leslie thought, instead of a plumber. When they went to the library together, he always looked for books about history or inventions.

It sure would be great if he were here now, going to work to fix pipes, stop leaks in bathrooms, or put rest rooms in new buildings. But Papa's job ended when the shop he worked for closed because they couldn't get the supplies they needed. His boss, Mr. Zambi, joined the Seabees. Papa said that was a good idea—Mr. Zambi could go on being a plumber.

For a short while, Papa looked for work. Then he joined the Seabees, too. "Sooner or later the draft will get around to me," he said. "I might as well stick with the work I know."

After Papa left, Mama applied for a job. "We'll need more than a navy allotment check to get by on," she said.

It would be great, too, if Mama were the way she used to be. Now she was busy, busy, busy—going to work, keeping house, volunteering for home-front tasks.

"Rotten war," Leslie muttered as she put the roses

in the blue vase. Then she and Kenny sat down to breakfast. Neither spoke, and the only sound they made was the crunching of cornflakes.

She ate hurriedly, then tackled her homework while Kenny dawdled over his breakfast. Concentrating really hard, she suddenly saw her error and solved the problems quickly. Satisfied, she stacked her books and gathered up the dishes. "Come on," she told Kenny, "get ready for school."

Kenny nodded, groaning. When they were about to leave, Leslie said, "Brush your hair out of your eyes." He did. It bounced right back. Then he jammed on a battered old baseball cap, which he wore everywhere.

Leslie pulled on her jacket and opened the door. "Whoops!" She almost banged into Ruthie, who was standing there with her hand up as though ready to knock.

"How come you're not at work?" Leslie knew she was blunt.

A line between Ruthie's brows deepened and her eyes looked heavy. "I've got the worst headache. I called in sick. Do you have any aspirin in the house?"

"Sure, come in." Leslie set her books on a chair. She'd be civil if it killed her. Sometimes she wished Ruthie would be nasty so she'd have a real reason to dislike her. Again, she had to admit she was jealous.

She found the aspirin.

"Thanks," Ruthie said. "Now I'm going back to bed."

"Guess what?" Kenny piped up. "Papa's coming home."

Ruthie's face brightened. "Really? When?"

"In two and a half weeks," Kenny told her. "And I'm going to practice my pitching like mad."

"I'll have to hurry to finish his sweater."

Leslie clenched her fists at her sides. "I knew she'd say that," she told herself. "I just knew it. Her and that dumb old sweater." But she also knew Papa would make a fuss over it.

Ruthie was still smiling. "If my headache gets better soon, I'll have almost all day to knit."

She gave them a little wave and ran down the steps.

"Come on," Leslie told Kenny, "we'd better hurry. And don't forget, after school we have to go to Benjamin's."

"I'm not going to any old store," Kenny stated flatly.

"Yes, you are. Meet me right in front of school as soon as you get out. We mustn't lose any time."

Kenny sulked for a full block.

Leslie's thoughts returned to Papa. "I wish I could do something special," she said.

"For what?"

"For Papa when he comes home." She paused. "We could hang out the flag."

Kenny said, "We do have his little flag in the window."

"That's his service flag. I mean the big one." As soon as she'd said the words, the idea didn't seem so great. Everybody flew the flag on holidays. She wanted something different for Papa, more exciting. Even before the war, flags were hung all over on Memorial Day, Flag Day, and the Fourth of July.

And Papa had the habit of saying, "Hang out the flag" whenever they did something he didn't think they were going to do. She always knew he'd say it if she didn't talk too long on the phone or if Kenny ate all his carrots at supper. Other people might say, "Hurray for you" or "It's about time," but Papa always laughed and said, "Hang out the flag."

Well, Ruthie would have her sweater for him, and Kenny would show him how well he could pitch. But what would she do? Just sit there like a lump and say things like, "I love you, Papa. I'm glad you're home"? She'd be a creep. She'd just have to think up something more special than hanging out the flag, as usual.

But one thing she *did* decide—she was going to find out what Buddy meant about a Nazi in Emmetsville.

2

After school, Kenny was still stubborn about going to the store. "Why do I have to go? Why can't I just go home?"

"Because I have to keep an eye on you."

Just then some kids passed them. A heavyset boy bumped into Leslie. It was Buddy Haver—who else?

"Okay, Buddy," she said, "we know you're here."

Lumbering after the kids, Buddy yelled, "Hey, guys, wait up." But the boys didn't stop for him, and he slowed down.

No matter how mad Leslie got at him sometimes, she still felt sorry for him. She knew how he must feel when the boys ignored him. There were two girls who always snubbed her. Once, when she got a much better grade than they, they laughed and chanted, "Brain, brain, down the drain."

She glanced toward Buddy, moving slowly ahead, and wished she could ask him about Oscar. But there were too many kids around. Anyway, right now she had to get to the store.

The day was warm and soft as she and Kenny hurried up the street. Like so many midwestern towns, Emmetsville was flat, and Benjamin's was only about six blocks from school. Kenny saw a late-in-the-season bumblebee and wanted to stop and watch it.

"No," Leslie told him, "we can't stop."

Then they passed an apartment house. The tree bank in front of it had been turned into a victory garden where dead tomato stalks and dried cucumber vines from the summer crop tangled with one another. Though only four feet wide, this was the nearest plot of ground the tenants could use for planting. Some people used vacant lots to raise corn and potatoes for their families. People called these plots victory gardens because they helped the war effort. So much food was needed for the armed forces that the government asked everyone to raise as much as they could for themselves. Thank goodness, Leslie thought, they had a backyard were Mama could grow vegetables.

Kenny walked a little faster, but then he started to count service flags in the windows. Almost every house had a little square white flag with a star for each person in the family who was serving in the armed forces. "Oh, there's three in that house." Kenny pointed. "And one star is yellow."

"It's gold," Leslie corrected him. "Somebody in that family was killed in the war."

A little farther on, they heard the clink of dishes in a coffee shop, where a waitress cleared a table near an open window. Leslie wished they didn't have to hurry so, but when they neared a stationery store, she slowed down. The door was ajar and, for a moment, she enjoyed the smell of books and paper and ink and the woodsy smell of lead pencils. She breathed deeply. Then, remembering their errand, she quickened her pace again.

When they reached Benjamin's hosiery department, there was a line to greet them—all women.

Kenny groaned. "Do we have to stand in line?"

"Yes." Leslie hated it as much as he did, but the line was short and kept moving. The only trouble Leslie had was keeping Kenny near her.

"Stay here," she hissed at him. "I'm not going to go looking for you later."

Glancing around the department, Leslie noticed a life-size cutout of Betty Grable, the pinup girl. It must be great, she thought, to go overseas to entertain the troops. Ever since the war started, Leslie had dreamed of being a Wac, a woman soldier, or a Wave, a woman sailor. She pictured herself doing brave things during battles. But the war would have to last seven more years for her to be old enough to join up. She certainly didn't want that.

Mama belonged to the AWVS, the American Women's Volunteer Service, but Leslie knew she was too young for that, too. She'd have to be satisfied with the home-front tasks she was doing.

Her daydream ended suddenly.

"Why are you children in line?" a haughty voice behind her asked.

Leslie turned and saw a tall, tight-lipped woman in a dark brown suit.

"I—I—we want to buy ladies' stockings." Leslie felt foolish as she looked down at her own saddle shoes and bobby socks.

"For your mother?"

"Yes."

"Well, if she wants them she should have come for them herself." The woman sniffed and looked away.

Leslie felt small and stupid. "She's—" She started to say Mama was at work but decided not to. Let the snooty thing wonder about it.

A few minutes later, Leslie was taking her turn at the counter. "Sun beige, size nine," she said quickly. That was what Mama always asked for when buying stockings.

"I'm sorry," the gray-haired saleslady said, "but we

only sell hosiery to adults when the supply is short."
She looked across Leslie's head to the snobbish woman
behind her.

"They're for my mother," Leslie said. "She's an
adult."

"I'm sorry," the saleslady said again. "Now please
step out of the way."

Leslie grabbed Kenny's arm and pulled him toward
the door. A march, "The Stars and Stripes Forever,"
was blaring from the music department. She stomped
her feet in time with it. Outside, she started for home
so fast that Kenny had to hurry to keep up with her.

"I'm so mad, I could knock a building over," she
said.

"Me, too," Kenny added.

At home, Leslie flopped down on the living room
sofa. Failure at anything really bugged her. Going into
the store to buy a pair of stockings for Mama was
such a little thing, and she couldn't even do that. Of
course Ruthie would have been able to get them if she
didn't work the same hours as Mama—or if she
weren't home sick.

"I'm going to call Tony," Kenny said. Tony was his
closest friend.

"Well, don't talk all day," Leslie told him. "What
if Papa tries to call?" The thought warmed her, but

deep down she knew Papa wouldn't call until Mama came home from work.

She could hear Kenny mumbling into the phone. Then he called to her. "Leslie, Tony says the school collections for the pennants are this Saturday."

"This Saturday!" She sat up straight. "No, they're next week." What else could go wrong?

Kenny did some more mumbling. Then he called to her again. "No, Tony says it's this Saturday."

Leslie hurried to the phone. "Tell him you'll call him right back. I have to call Mary."

Kenny backed up, holding tightly to the receiver. "Come on," she said, "I'll give it right back to you." She grabbed the phone from him and dialed quickly.

She hoped Mary was at home. Mary was.

"Hi. It's Leslie. When is the school contest at the collection center?"

"Saturday," Mary answered.

"This Saturday? I thought it wasn't until next week."

"No," Mary said. "A notice was put on the bulletin board this morning in the hall. I hope our room wins all the pennants."

"Same here," Leslie said. "Thanks. See you. Bye."

Her mind was racing. She remembered that she and Kenny had gotten a late start that morning because of Ruthie. They had reached school just in time. She hadn't looked at the bulletin board. After school, she had hurried, too. Probably, before the end of the week, all the teachers would remind their students of the contest. They had been doing so since the war began. They would tell the pupils to collect all the newspapers, cooking grease, and tin cans they could. Each room would try to win the little felt pennants by turning in the most.

Leslie gave the phone back to Kenny. "Tell Tony good-bye. We have to tie up the papers in the garage."

When the contests had started, Leslie and Kenny had asked their neighbors to save newspapers for them. The neighbors had said, "Sure," but then had just put them in the garage in loose piles. Leslie and Kenny had to tie them in bundles. They each would take half of the papers and half of the tin cans to the collection center. They took turns contributing the grease Mama saved in a jar. This time it was Kenny's turn.

They had just tied the last bundle of papers when they saw Mama come down the sidewalk from the trolley stop at the corner. They ran to meet her.

"I thought the school contest was next week," Leslie told her, "but it's this coming Saturday."

Mama smiled, looking down the driveway. "Well, I see you have the papers all stacked out of the way of the car. We won't have to move them when we go for groceries on Thursday."

"But we have to jump on the cans," Kenny said. He was always eager to flatten the tin cans as they were told to do.

"You will do that after supper," Mama told him. "Now tell me," she said, her eyes filled with hope, "did you have any luck getting my stockings?"

"No luck, Mama," Leslie told her. "There were some rayons left, but they wouldn't sell them to me because I'm not an adult." She remembered how small the saleslady had made her feel and squirmed uneasily. Watching Mama's shoulders slump, she became angry again. "What's that got to do with it?"

"Oh, they get complaints, I guess." Mama sounded weary. "People get peeved when they miss out on the merchandise."

They went inside. Mama sat down heavily on the sofa. Her light hair curled on her forehead where it escaped her hairpins. She smoothed it back with both palms. "I had so hoped to get a pair. When Papa comes home, we'll want to celebrate, and I have only mended rayons."

Leslie had often seen Mama sewing the runs.

"We can try again," Leslie offered. "Maybe if you give me a note . . ." They had accounts at both of the main stores in town.

"Yes, that's a good idea," Mama said, getting to her feet. "I'll write one right now. Then you'll have it ready the next time you try."

As she walked to the desk in the corner of the living room, Kenny tagged after her. "Why don't you paint your legs, Mama?" he asked. "Tony's mother does."

Mama laughed. "No, I can't get leg makeup on right."

"Well, there's always the black market," Leslie said. "Mary's aunt gets nylons there six pairs at a time."

"Where's the black market?" Kenny wanted to know.

Mama patted his head. "Anywhere someone can sell something against the law."

Leslie felt guilty for having suggested such a thing. "It's almost like helping the Nazis," she muttered.

Then Mama added, "Even if I wanted to, I couldn't pay their prices." She wrote quickly and handed the note to Leslie. It read, "Please give a pair of stockings—nylon or rayon—sun beige, size nine, to my daughter and charge to my account. Jane (Mrs. Edgar) Jamieson."

Leslie took the note to the clothes tree in the hallway and shoved it into a pocket of her jacket. Then she went into the kitchen, where Mama was putting a casserole into the oven.

Leslie thought briefly about Oscar Von Desch. Then

she reminded herself that she didn't even know which Oscar Buddy was calling a Nazi. There must be more than one in Emmetsville.

"But Papa is more important," she told herself. "I must think of a great welcome home for him." She would concentrate on that—she really would.

3

Leslie wondered how many days there were in a leave. "How long can Papa stay home?" she asked Mama at supper.

"He gets here early Sunday and stays until Friday morning."

Five full days, Leslie counted. "If we hang out the flag for Papa when he comes home, can we leave it out all the time he's here?"

"I don't think so," Mama said as she cut a slice of store-bought cake for each of them. "You have to take it in at night and when it rains."

There went Leslie's grand idea where the flag was concerned. If she had to take it in just as at other times, there'd be nothing special about it.

After she and Kenny did the dishes, Kenny headed for the back porch. "Come on," he said, "let's jump on the cans."

The first thing Kenny did was stomp each foot down hard on the side of a can so that it curled up around his heel. Then he clomped around, lining up his share of the cans on the back step. When they were divided evenly—one bunch for him and one for Leslie—he removed the cans from his heels and proceeded to stomp on the rest.

Mama came to the door. "Could you be a little more quiet," she told Kenny. "It sounds like a boiler factory back here. I want to turn on the news."

Leslie squashed her cans as quickly and quietly as she could. Usually she used a can opener and cut out both ends so that she could flatten them more neatly. But now that seemed like too much bother. She took her bag of cans to the garage and placed it beside the tied-up papers. Then she went inside. Kenny followed.

She wished they could just forget about the collections until Papa's leave was over. Patiently she waited until the news program was ended.

Mama flicked off the radio, shaking her head. "There's such terrible fighting in Italy—around a place called Salerno."

Leslie shrugged. Always a new place. No wonder they call it a world war. Italy's in Europe, but there's Japan, too, and their crummy general. "Rotten Tojo," she muttered.

"Rotten Hitler," Kenny added, making it sound like a motto.

Leslie's thoughts went back to Papa's leave. "What

are we going to do while Papa is home?" she asked Mama.

"Well, he'll want to see Grandma." Papa's mother lived in Grosbank, thirty-five miles west of them. "I'm glad there's still some gas in the tank," Mama went on, "and we have one coupon left. That should be enough to get us there and back—even with three short trips for groceries."

Gas was one of the rationed things everyone complained about. Cabdrivers could get more for their cabs, and fishermen could get more for their boats. But if you didn't need it for your work, forget it.

All Mama needed it for was to go for groceries once a week and maybe do some errands around town. Leslie knew they could get more for an emergency, but Papa's coming home wasn't an emergency.

"I just hope the car holds up," Mama continued.

"Won't they have to make some new cars before the war is over?" Leslie asked. So many of the cars she saw on the street were old clunkers with lots of rust spots and dents, making loud chugging noises.

"I don't know," Mama answered, picking up her sewing basket. "But we couldn't buy one, anyway."

Just as Mama stuffed her darning egg into one of Kenny's socks, the phone rang. "I'll get it." Leslie leaped toward the phone just a second before Kenny did. "Hello. Yes, just a minute." She held out the receiver. "It's for you, Mama."

She had been wishing it were Mary. She felt like chatting. Then Kenny stood beside her, rattling the checkers box. "I'll beat you," he said.

"Okay. But only one game."

They had just begun when Mama hung up. She looked pleased about something.

"That was the file girl in our office," Mama said. "She heard the Circle Store might get some hosiery in on Thursday." Mama smiled. "She has friends in both department stores. So on Thursday, you will try again to get me a pair," she told Leslie.

"Sure, Mama."

"She also reminded me of the blackout tomorrow night," Mama added. "So get your homework done early."

The blackout! "Is it okay if I go with Mary and her mother on her rounds?" Mary's mother was an air-raid warden, a volunteer who patrolled the streets during blackouts to make sure that not a smidgeon of light showed. She had taken her husband's place when he went on the second shift at work.

"Can I go, too?" Kenny begged.

"Yes, you may go, Leslie, if your homework is done," Mama said, "but, Kenny, you stay home with me." When Kenny groaned, she added, "You wouldn't want me to stay home alone, would you?"

Kenny hesitated. "No-o, I guess not." Then he said quickly, "Maybe you could ask Ruthie to come over."

Leslie held her breath. She didn't want Kenny to go along. She had to put up with taking him everywhere while Mama was at work.

Mama shook her head. "I'm afraid not, but we can play the phonograph, and I'll make you a sandwich and Kool-Aid. We'll have a blackout party, the two of us."

Kenny's eyes lit up. "Okay."

Thank heavens, Leslie thought, that's settled. She wouldn't have to listen to Kenny pleading to go with her.

The next morning, when she met Mary in front of school, Leslie reminded her of the blackout and of her going along.

Mary bobbed her blond head up and down, smiling. She had a pointed little face and her smile spread across most of it. "Come over early," she said, "because my mother has to leave as soon as the blackout starts."

"I will," Leslie said.

As soon as the pupils were seated in the classroom, their teacher, Miss Ellinger, told them, "Don't forget the contest this Saturday at the collection center. Bring all your newspapers, tin cans, and grease so our room can win at least some of the pennants."

Immediately Buddy Haver raised his hand. Good heavens, Leslie thought, what can he say to make himself important about the collections? We've been having them since the war began.

"Yes, Buddy," Miss Ellinger said.

"My cousin just moved to the country and he collects milkweed pods for the war."

A couple of snickers sounded in the room.

"Don't laugh," Miss Ellinger said. "Buddy is right. Milkweed pods are being collected. The fluff inside them is used in life jackets for servicemen."

"If we could collect them"—Buddy was making the most of his information—"we could haul a truckload of them on our backs. They're light."

"Yes, they are," Miss Ellinger agreed.

Before she could go any further, Buddy said, "And my cousin has a beehive. They're saving the beeswax from the honeycombs, too."

More snickers. Leslie hoped he wouldn't blurt out his story about the Nazi in Emmetsville—although she was still interested in hearing more about it.

Miss Ellinger said, "Buddy's right again. The government wants beeswax for waterproofing ammo shells and some airplane surfaces." Then she hurried to say, "Now, I would like all of you to write an essay about a way to honor our servicemen."

"Like what?" Again, Buddy made himself heard.

"Anything you like. Just pretend it's for someone in your family who's in the service, maybe going overseas or coming home. Write what you would like to do for them." She smiled. "You have until Friday."

That wasn't as easy as it sounded, Leslie knew. She had been trying hard to think of something special to do for Papa, and her mind still went blank. To dream up another idea for an essay was too much. But whatever she decided for Papa could do for her essay, too.

After school, Leslie did her homework as fast as she could, all except the essay. She couldn't think of a thing beyond hanging out the flag. Boy, was she in a rut! But she hoped that by tomorrow evening, she would come up with a dazzling idea. When she did, putting it into an essay would be easy.

After supper, Leslie set out for Mary's house. Daylight was nearly gone. She knew that when the siren sounded, all the streetlights would go out. Every house would darken because of blackout curtains at the windows. If people had nothing to cover their windows with, they had to wait in the dark until it was over.

It was dark by the time Leslie reached Mary's house. Ten minutes later, the siren sounded.

"Come on, girls," Mary's mother said. She had on her air-raid warden helmet and a band on her arm. She carried a flashlight in case of emergency. "Get Jinco, Mary."

Jinco was a German shepherd. Mary's mother took him along for protection and Mary and Leslie for company.

Up and down the streets of their route they went. A car crept along without headlights on. At one house a sliver of light shone at the bottom of a window. Mary's mother knocked on the door. "Pull your window shade all the way down," she told the man who answered.

"Sure will. Sorry."

As they continued on their route, Jinco strained at his leash. Leslie helped Mary hang on to him. Barking, he tugged toward a small stone house. Who could be hiding in there? A spy? A deserter from the army? Leslie's mind went over pieces of war stories she had read. Suddenly a blur shot past them and she heard the snarl of an angry cat.

Mary slapped Jinco's back. "Stop. Behave," she said. Jinco settled down.

They were near the end of the street when they saw a small reddish light close to the ground. It grew dim, then glowed brightly, dimmed and brightened again. "Someone's smoking," Mary's mother said.

A few steps farther on, Leslie could make out the form of a man, sitting hunched over on the curb. When they came up to him she saw, in the gloom, that he was middle-aged and shabby. It was Mr. Gillis. Lately, people had begun calling him an old drunk.

"Mr. Gillis," Mary's mother told him, "you must put out your cigarette."

"Why?" His head wobbled as he looked up at her. "I lit it inside." He gestured toward the open door of his old frame house behind him.

"But the glow of your cigarette can be seen from far off. A Nazi or Jap pilot high in the air could spot it."

Mr. Gillis snorted. "Nazi or Jap! You crazy, lady? There's none of them around here." He stood up unsteadily.

"You must put it out, anyway." Mary's mother was firm. "The law says so."

Mr. Gillis took another puff and threw the cigarette into the gutter, where it sputtered and died. Then he reeled toward the doorway. "Japs at Bataan," he muttered. "Not here." He pulled the door shut after himself.

"His son was killed at Bataan," Mary's mother said in a low tone. "And his wife died soon afterward. Poor man."

They turned away to finish the rounds. The blackout

time, about thirty minutes, was nearly up when they headed back toward Mary's house.

Sitting on the darkened porch, Leslie asked Mary, "Did you write your essay yet?"

"No," Mary answered, "but I was thinking of singing. You know, have a group of kids sing for the wounded men in the hospital."

"But we don't have a military hospital here."

"You're right, but someone might come home wounded, or maybe the group could sing at a homecoming party for a soldier—or a going-away party."

"Yes, that's a good idea," Leslie agreed. "Now I have to think of one." She sighed.

Just then the siren sounded the all clear and the streetlights went on. Leslie got up to leave. All the way home, she thought of what she might do for Papa when he returned. Maybe she'd make a big Welcome sign for him, or maybe an oversized greeting card that all the neighbors could sign. Nah, neither idea was very exciting. And the thought of hanging out the flag came back—if she could just do it in a different way.

As she opened the front door, she heard Mama and Kenny singing along with the phonograph record, "Bless 'em all, bless 'em all. The long and the short and the tall . . ."

She gave Mama a little wave as she went in. Then she flopped down on the sofa until the song ended.

"Now let's put on 'When the Lights Go On Again All Over the World,' " Kenny said, hunting through the pile of records. "It's a good blackout song."

Mama laughed. "The blackout is over and I think we sang enough." She sounded tired. "Put the records away. It's time to get ready for bed."

Kenny groaned, then turned to Leslie. "Did anything happen on your rounds?"

"Sure, a Jap plane swooped down and blew the end of the town off the map." Then she laughed and wondered why.

"That's nothing to joke about," Mama said, frowning.

"I know." Leslie thought of Papa. Maybe he'd be sent to a place where towns would be blown up. And the blackouts would be real, not just practice ones like here. "It was a dumb thing to say."

A slight knock sounded on the front door and Ruthie came rushing in. "Aunt Jane, could I see one of Papa's sweaters so I could measure mine against it?" She held up the unfinished sweater she was making. It was gray with a red stripe around the middle.

Leslie clenched her fists and looked away. And I still haven't even started anything, she thought.

"Certainly," Mama told Ruthie. She turned to Kenny. "Run upstairs and get Papa's brown sweater."

Ruthie beamed and swished back her blond hair. "I hope Papa will like mine."

Suddenly Leslie felt she'd explode if she held in her feelings one more moment. "Why do you always call him Papa? He's not your father. You call Mama aunt. Why don't you call Papa uncle?"

Mama glared at her. "There's no call for that, Leslie."

Ruthie's eyes widened. "Oh. You—you don't mind, do you, Aunt Jane?"

"Certainly not," Mama answered. "Leslie shouldn't have said that."

"No, I guess I shouldn't have," Leslie half apologized, tossing her head. She couldn't let go of her resentment. "Anyway, when I learn to knit, I'll learn cable stitch. It makes sweaters much better-looking."

Mama glared again.

Kenny came bouncing in with Papa's brown sweater. Ruthie measured the length of hers against it. "Good. I'm closer to finishing it than I thought. Thanks, Aunt Jane." She left immediately.

Mama glanced at the clock. "It's getting close to your bedtime," she said, nodding to Leslie and Kenny.

Thank heavens, Mama isn't making a fuss about the way I acted toward Ruthie, Leslie thought as she helped Kenny put the records away. She was sorry about her outburst, but she was still annoyed at Ruthie and more determined than ever to have something extra special for Papa when he came home—something better than Ruthie's sweater.

Maybe she could make a giant flag for him. That's silly, she thought, I'm no Betsy Ross. Besides, she had only two weeks.

4

The first thing Leslie thought when she woke was, This is Thursday. She had to try to get Mama some stockings at the Circle Store today. At least she had Mama's note. But she dreaded the errand. She'd feel like two cents again if the salesclerk told her to leave the line.

The very thought made her peevish and short with Kenny. When she opened the little tub of margarine at breakfast, she snapped, "It was your turn to color it."

He usually loved to press the capsule of orange food coloring through the white margarine to make it look like butter, which was hard to get.

"I forgot. Eat it that way."

"No, it looks like lard on the bread. It turns my stomach." She pushed the tub away and ate her toast plain.

On the way to school, she reminded Kenny of their errand.

Kenny's usual groan came before he asked, "Do I have to go?"

"Yes." She wasn't going to say any more. If she did, she'd have to listen to more of his complaining.

In class, Leslie was surprised when Miss Ellinger said twelve essays had already been handed in. The rest would have to be in by tomorrow.

"We have three essays by boys," Miss Ellinger said, "all differently written, about going on a picnic with the servicemen."

Just like boys, Leslie thought, always thinking of their stomachs. There was nothing very special about that. But so far her idea of the flag was nothing special, either. If she stuck with it, it would have to be an extraordinary flag. "And we have two about forming a chorus," Miss Ellinger went on, "to sing for the boys going away or coming home."

Leslie stole a look at Mary. Mary grinned. One of those two essays was hers. She must have written it after the blackout last night.

"And we have three students who think a parade would be nice," Miss Ellinger continued. "The rest would like to have parties." She stacked the papers neatly on her desk. "We cannot act on all of the suggestions, but it would be nice if we could arrange something that you wrote about."

Miss Ellinger paused, then smiled. "And now I have

a surprise for you. A half hour before the closing bell, we will have a visitor. Sergeant Thorne, a neighbor of mine, will be coming to see us."

Excitement spread through the room like a streak of lightning.

"Quiet, please," Miss Ellinger said. "We have to hurry through our other classes in order to finish on time."

It was two-thirty when the officer arrived. He grinned at the class. "Hi. I'm Sergeant Arthur Thorne. I'm in the army air force."

Buddy Haver was frantically waving his hand. Miss Ellinger was giving him a warning glance and looking embarrassed at the same time.

Then Buddy said loudly, "My father is in the air force."

"Well, good for him," the sergeant said. "Are there any more of you who have family members in the air force?"

Two boys stood up and said that their brothers were.

"Well, good for them," the sergeant said again.

Leslie wished a Seabee officer had come to the school. But she certainly wouldn't have tried to get all the attention, the way Buddy had.

Then the sergeant asked, "How many of you would like to be in one of the services?"

All the boys' hands shot up. So did some of the

girls'. Again Buddy called out, this time without even raising his hand, "I'd like to be a fly-boy like my father."

Leslie felt like throwing up. Then she had to grin. She could picture Buddy's clumsy feet clomping along at drill as he tried to keep in step.

The sergeant didn't ask any more questions. Instead he told them about himself and his life in the service. The time went quickly, and suddenly the bell was ringing. The sergeant shook Miss Ellinger's hand and said she had a fine group of pupils. Then, with a little salute, he left.

Outside, Buddy and the other boys, bunched on the sidewalk, were extra noisy. "I'm going to be a fly-boy like my father," Buddy said, raising his voice to be heard. Then he put his books on the curb and spread out his arms like wings. He ran around in a circle, making a zoom-zoom sound.

Leslie felt like telling him his father only had a desk job at the air base. She had overheard his mother telling Mama. But let him act dumb if he wanted to.

Then one of the girls asked, "Is your father really a pilot, Buddy?"

Buddy stopped his circling and kept his face turned away as he gathered up his books. "No, not really, not yet." He didn't look at anyone as he answered.

Leslie was glad she hadn't said anything smart to him. He was just trying to act important, as usual. She often wished she were important, too. Everybody had a right to dream.

As she waited for Kenny, Buddy started to get loud again. She wondered what he was bragging about now. Then, without intending to eavesdrop, she heard him say, "Well, I know one Nazi."

There he goes again, she thought. But she listened.

"Who?" several voices chorused.

"Old Oscar Von Desch. He's from Germany."

"Aw, you're crazy," came the same chorus of voices.

So Buddy did mean Mr. Von Desch, Leslie thought. But old? He was only about thirty-five. He was a tall, square-faced, light-haired man who spoke with an accent and never smiled, and his thrown-back shoulders always looked as though someone had just yelled, "Attention!"

Leslie thought of his wife. Mrs. Von Desch was always nice when they passed on the street or met in a store. The Von Desches lived in the last house on the southern end of Laramie Street. It was an old, dark brown, two-story house set way back from the sidewalk. It had bushes growing along the path up to the front door and several other bushes clustered on the lawn.

The house had a silent, deserted look, and Leslie

often wondered why the Von Desches had always kept to themselves so much. Why did they avoid other people?

She was still waiting for Kenny when the group of kids melted away. Buddy had hung back. Now she and Buddy were the only ones left.

He stepped over to her. "Want to go to Von Desch's place and see I'm right about him?" he asked. She knew he was hurt because the kids had scoffed. "He talks on a shortwave radio or something in German."

"Who said so?"

"Somebody I know."

"Who?" She didn't believe him any more than the other kids did.

"Pete from Benjamin's shoe department. I heard him telling someone. They didn't know I was on the other side of the shoe rack." Buddy leaned closer. "But don't tell anybody I told you."

Good gosh! Leslie thought. He's blabbing all over about everything and then says don't tell anyone. But she agreed. "Okay. I don't believe it, anyhow."

"Well, come on, I'll show you. They said he has a shortwave in the cellar. We could sneak to the back of the house and look in the window."

"I can't." Leslie almost wished she could. What if Buddy was telling the truth? To help catch a spy—

that would really be doing something for the war effort. It would outshine Ruthie's sweater anytime. "I have to go to the store for my mother."

"Well, how about tomorrow?"

"Maybe. I'll see."

Kenny ran toward them. "I had to stay in," he said. "I talked in class."

"Come on," Leslie told Kenny, "we have to hurry." She turned to Buddy. "See you tomorrow."

On the way to the store, she thought of Oscar Von Desch. Her family had met him and his wife once in a while at school functions like the Christmas play and the ice cream festival. The Von Desches were very proud of a skinny little boy with blond, curly hair. He was their nephew. He was in Leslie's grade at school, but he had quit school in the middle of the term two years ago, right after Pearl Harbor. No one knew why. They said he went back to live with his parents. When Leslie ran into Mrs. Von Desch one day and asked where his parents lived, Mrs. Von Desch had said, "In another state." Leslie hadn't had the nerve to ask which one.

Now Kenny was saying, "There it is," as he pointed to a two-story building with a huge gold circle mounted on the front edge of the flat roof. Inside the circle, the word *store* was spelled out. It reminded

Leslie of a branding iron, which she'd seen in a western movie.

Several women waited their turn at the hosiery counter.

"Another line," Kenny said.

"It's moving," Leslie said. "We won't have to wait long." She clutched Mama's note, hoping the clerk wouldn't say that she sold stockings only to adults. Soon Leslie found herself third in line. The woman being waited on asked for size 10.

"I'm sorry, there's only one pair left. It's size 9½."

"I'll take it," the woman said quickly.

Not again! Leslie thought.

The saleslady finished waiting on the woman and then raised her hand for attention. "I'm sorry, ladies, but that was the last pair. We'll be getting more in—"

"When?" an angry voice cut in. It belonged to the woman directly in front of Leslie.

"I'm—I'm not—sure," the saleslady stammered. "Our orders don't come in regularly."

Leslie put Mama's note back into her pocket. "Come on," she told Kenny.

On the way home, they passed a billboard with a painting of Uncle Sam pointing his finger. "I want you," he was saying. Leslie looked away. She had seen that picture so many times in newspapers, magazines, and on posters in the post office. The billboard held the biggest one, though. The biggest! That was it—a flag painted on a billboard for Papa. Maybe you shouldn't let a cloth flag hang out at night or in the rain, but if it's painted on a ship or a plane—or a billboard—it can stay out in all kinds of weather. After all her concentration, the idea had jumped out at her by itself.

Excited, Leslie began to hurry.

"Don't go so fast," Kenny said. "I'm tired." But he kept up with her.

At home, she went right to work on her essay. She called it "The Flag They're Fighting For" and wrote about painting a huge flag on a billboard to honor the servicemen. Only, in her heart, it would be for Papa.

The last words of her essay were, "If they are fighting for our country, they are fighting for our flag. And if they fight to keep our flag flying, it should be theirs—as big and as bold as we can make it for them." She patted the paper, satisfied, and put it in her notebook.

When Mama came home, she was naturally disappointed about the stockings. "Well, next Tuesday, Benjamin's might have some more," she said, walking into the kitchen.

Trailing after her, Kenny asked, "What's for supper?"

"Pepper pot," Mama told him. "And don't turn your nose up. I can get tripe easier than other meat."

"Yuck!" Kenny turned right around and went back into the living room.

But Leslie wouldn't have cared, at that moment, if she had to eat a bushel of tripe. Her essay was finished, and she loved what she'd written. Then she heard Mama say, "I think we'll wait until tomorrow evening to go for the groceries. I have so many other things to do tonight." Mama gestured toward the little stack of bills to be sorted out and letters to be answered.

At supper, Leslie's thoughts wandered back to Buddy's blabbing. He could be right. And if he was, he and she were the only kids in on it. The others didn't believe him.

She wondered if Mama had heard anything. "Mama, remember Oscar Von Desch?" she began. "People say he's a Nazi."

Mama said, "Really?"

"Yes," Leslie went on. "Do you think we should report him to the police?"

Mama's eyes widened. She rested her fork on her plate. "No, indeed, you should not. You're not sure. You could hurt people by doing something like that."

"But, Mama, if he's a Nazi, don't you think he should be reported?"

"Yeah, let's tell the FBI," Kenny cut in, "and then we can kick him out of the country."

Mama held up her hands. "Stop that, both of you. Mr. Von Desch is German and he has an accent, but how do you know he's a Nazi?"

Leslie had to admit she didn't know. And she certainly didn't want to hurt anyone. She'd always thought she would like to be a newspaper reporter, but the idea of digging up someone's past life and scandal went against her. Families could be hurt. She'd rather make up stories and write books. Anyway, Buddy was probably only trying, as usual, to make himself look important.

Leslie found it hard to fall asleep that night. Her thoughts kept darting from her essay to Von Desch to Papa's leave and back again. She heard Mama try the front door to see if it was locked, and then she heard Mama's steps on the stairs. She heard the click of the switch as Mama turned off the hallway light and Mama's door softly closing.

Leslie got up. Maybe Mama would like to talk. Leslie knew Mama missed Papa, so she must miss talking to him before going to bed every night.

When she knocked, Mama said, "Come in."

Entering, Leslie saw Mama holding Papa's picture and smiling at the smile Papa wore. He was in uniform.

Mama looked across at her. "Yes, Leslie?"

Suddenly Leslie felt she was intruding. Mama would probably rather be alone with her thoughts. "I was just going to talk, but it's late. Nothing important, anyhow." She put her hand on the doorknob.

"Yes, it is late," Mama agreed softly. "Good-night, dear."

5

On Friday morning, all the essays but two had been handed in.

"The students who haven't done their essays have one more chance," Miss Ellinger told them. "They may try to write them at lunchtime."

She riffled through the papers in her hand. "I think we should act on some of these. It may be a little late for a school picnic, but the ideas of the students who wrote about them are good, and some of the food they suggested could be used at parties." She paused a moment. "Maybe we could arrange an after-school party for Anne's brother, who is coming home on furlough."

Everyone clapped.

Leslie thought, Papa is coming home on leave, too. But she hadn't told Miss Ellinger. Anyway, she wouldn't want her teacher to have to worry about two parties at the same time.

"And a parade," Miss Ellinger was saying. "Well,

on Armistice Day our room could join the end of the parade and march down Main Street."

Again, everyone clapped and cheered.

"But that won't be until November eleventh." A few moans sounded.

"And we could get a group together to sing. My own brother is leaving in three weeks for the army air force." Miss Ellinger looked sad for a moment, then smiled and looked proud. "I'd like it if you all could learn "Off We Go into the Wild Blue Yonder" and come to our house to sing it for him."

More claps and cheers.

"All the essays are good, and you'll get good marks for them." She put the papers on her desk and went on with the class.

Leslie was crushed. Didn't Miss Ellinger think her idea was good enough to act on?

She tried to put her mind on the rules of grammar Miss Ellinger was teaching, but she couldn't. She was glad when the lunch bell rang. She shoved her books and papers into her desk and picked up her lunch bag. But she didn't feel very much like eating.

"Leslie," Miss Ellinger said, "I want to see you a moment before you leave."

Now what? Leslie wondered. Well, no matter, she couldn't feel much worse than she did at that moment. She caught Mary's questioning look and shrugged.

After the other students had all filed out, Leslie went to the front of the room.

Miss Ellinger was smiling. "Leslie, I thought your idea was fine and well written. But I didn't mention it to the class because we have some impetuous boys who might end up in the police station for trying to paint over advertisements on billboards." She rolled her eyes upward.

"Like Buddy," Leslie couldn't help saying.

"Yes," Miss Ellinger agreed, laughing. "But you can look into it yourself. Maybe volunteers are allowed to do something like that." She patted Leslie's shoulder and led her toward the door. "I'll inquire around, too. We'll see."

Leslie's heart beat fast. Her idea was a good one.

In the lunch room, she told Mary about her essay and what Miss Ellinger had said about keeping it quiet. "Do you know any billboard owners I could ask?"

"No," Mary answered. "But maybe you could find one in the phone book."

"I could try." Then Leslie had an idea. "Do you think there'd be a phone number on the billboard?"

Mary's little face puckered in thought. "I think the only number would belong to the company advertising on it."

"I guess you're right. I wish I could see one right

now." She caught Mary's arm. "How about walking over to Leland Street after school? I saw one there yesterday."

Mary shook her head. "I have to go right home. My mother wants me to help her clean upstairs."

"That's okay," Leslie said. Then she added, "I'm glad we're going to sing."

Mary beamed at her. "So am I. But I wonder if Miss Ellinger's brother's going away will be our first time."

After school, Leslie looked for Kenny. She saw a group of boys, their books and coats on the ground nearby. They were prancing around, darting at one another with their hands to their heads and fingers pointing like horns. Bullfighters! Leslie guessed she'd find Kenny in the midst of them. She did, and just as she was going toward him, Buddy stepped in front of her.

"How about it? Are you going to"—he looked around to see if anyone could hear—"to Von Desch's with me?"

Leslie had almost forgotten. "I have to do something first. And I have to get Kenny home. If he can play with Tony, I can go."

"You really will?"

She knew it was a surprise to Buddy that anyone would agree to join him in anything. "Sure, come to my place in about an hour." She still didn't believe him, but if what he said was true, she'd hate to miss anything.

"Okay." He walked off.

Leslie had something else to think of right then— the billboard. She caught Kenny's wrist and told him they had to leave.

He protested. "I'm not going to any old store."

"No, not today. But I have to look at something."

Slowly, Kenny gathered up his jacket and books and then slapped on his baseball cap. "Where are we going?"

"Leland Street."

"Why?" Kenny wanted to know.

"You'll see."

Kenny fell silent and just poked along behind her. Leslie kept a sharp lookout for other billboards but didn't see any. Finally she paused before the one on Leland Street. It was as high as the roof of the one-story building beside it.

Kenny looked up at Uncle Sam's picture. "Are you going to join the army?"

"Don't be silly."

"Well, why did we have to hike over here?"

"To see this billboard."

"Why?"

Leslie didn't answer. She was too disappointed. There was some small printing at the lower-right-hand corner, but it was too high to read.

"This is goofy," Kenny told her. "Why didn't we go look at the one near Tony's house?"

"Near Tony's house?"

"Yeah. Why did we have to walk over here?"

"Come on." Leslie started off, heading back toward home. Tony's house was just a block beyond theirs. His older brother always rushed him home right after school, so Kenny seldom got a chance to walk with him.

When they neared the billboard on Tony's street, they found two men in white overalls and caps putting up a new advertisement about face soap—"to bring out the beauty of your skin." One man finished the corner with a slap and push of a wide brush on a piece of a lady's picture. The edges met perfectly.

When the two men climbed down, one went right to a truck at the curb. He barely looked at Leslie and Kenny.

The other man was younger. He had straw-colored hair and blue eyes and a slight limp. Grinning at them, he said, "Hi, kids."

Kenny answered, "Hi."

Leslie twisted a strand of hair nervously, then caught herself and stopped. She tried to be casual.

"Must people pay to put something on the billboard?"

"Bet your boots they do," the man said. "Why? You going to advertise something?" He smiled again, but his voice wasn't smart-alecky. He wasn't making fun of her.

"No-o," she answered, wondering if she should tell him. Then she plunged in. "We want a big flag painted on a billboard for my father. He's in the Seabees and he's coming home on leave."

"Well, you tell him hi for me. I was in the navy, too, but not the Seabees division."

"Why did you quit?" Kenny asked point-blank.

"I didn't. My ship was torpedoed and I got smashed up. Got pins in my leg."

"Oh." Leslie cringed.

Again, the man grinned. "So you want a big flag for your father? That's a dandy idea. But"—he scratched his jaw—"that will cost money."

"Even if volunteers do it?" Leslie asked.

"Yep. The billboard company rents the space." He paused a moment. "But maybe you could find someone to let you paint it on a garage or a barn or something. I'd volunteer to help. I like to paint."

"Gee, thanks." Then Leslie pointed to the side of the truck. Beneath the words Outdoor Advertising there was a phone number. She memorized it. "Could I call you there if I find a place?"

"Sure thing. Just ask for Dave."

"Thanks. My name's Leslie and this is Kenny."

Dave nodded. "Glad to know you. So long for now." Then he got into the truck, and it moved away.

Leslie remembered Mama and Papa always saying, "Never talk to strangers." She shouldn't, but this was different. Besides, she didn't intend to go anywhere with strangers, or let Kenny go.

Looking after the truck, Kenny said, "I like Dave. Maybe I could ask him to pitch to me like Papa did."

Leslie jotted the phone number on the truck in her notebook in case she forgot it.

"Let's look for a garage right now," Kenny said.

"Sure, come on."

They scouted around the area on their way home. Not far from their house, they found one. The owner was cleaning dead stalks out of his victory garden, which took up a corner of his well-kept lawn. He must be a particular man, Leslie thought. Not a blade of grass was out of place. The garage was painted sparkling white and had a nice outside wall.

When Leslie said, "Hello," the balding man looked annoyed.

"Yes, what is it?"

Leslie was about to back off. Then she thought, he can't kill me for asking. It was just what she wanted.

The garage was not behind the house, like theirs was, and its wall could be seen from the street.

"May we paint a flag on the side of your garage?" There, she had said it.

"Paint on my garage? I should say not. Now get out of here and stop bothering folks who have work to do." He turned his back to them and bent over his garden.

"Boy, he's a real crab," Kenny whispered.

"Shh," Leslie warned him and, grabbing his sleeve, tugged him after her.

6

They were going through their front door when Leslie remembered Buddy. She wondered if she should skip meeting him, then decided not to. She looked at Kenny.

"Do you want to play at Tony's place?" she asked him.

"Sure. I can practice my pitching." He raced to the back porch for his ball and glove.

"Okay, but don't stay too long. And stay at his house. No wandering around. Then come straight home."

"Okay." He was out the door before she could say anything further. And in less than ten minutes, she heard Buddy's knock.

Buddy had his collar turned up and his cap pulled so far down over his brow, he could hardly see. What a dumb spy he'd make, Leslie thought.

"We'll have to hurry," she told him. "My mother will be home from work soon."

They rushed the three and one-half blocks to the

end of the street. Easing themselves in through Von Desch's gate, they crossed the lawn and sneaked along the side of the house. Close to the back corner was a small cellar window. The high hedge along the fence on all sides gave the house a closed-off look. All was quiet and sort of spooky.

"Look, he's in the cellar now," Buddy whispered, pointing to the slit of light at the top of the small window.

"Shh, he might hear you," Leslie said. To get caught there was all they needed!

They tiptoed toward the window. When they reached it, Leslie could see that the dark paper pasted on the pane for blackouts had curled down at one corner and across the top. The glass had been broken and a small piece had fallen out. They had to hunch down to peer through. With her eye to the corner of the window, Leslie could easily see Von Desch at a speaker of some kind. It must be the shortwave thing Buddy had spoken about. Von Desch was switching something on and off the way soldiers did in the movies when they wanted to talk to their officers on the battlefields. His voice came to her, but not too clearly.

"He's talking German," Buddy whispered.

Leslie signaled Buddy to be quiet. Von Desch *was* speaking German, but she couldn't understand the language. He could have been ordering potatoes from a market, for all she knew. Then the word *oferdon* reached her. That sounded like the name of the steel company Mama worked for—Overton—pronounced with a German accent.

Leslie decided to keep it to herself. She wouldn't want to trust Buddy with it, not yet, anyway. Before she could hear anything more, Buddy motioned that it was his turn at the tiny peephole. She nodded. He was squatting and tried to scoot over to her place when he lost his balance and fell back heavily against an old drainpipe at the corner of the house. The metallic crunch sounded loud, and Leslie caught a fleeting glimpse of Von Desch jerking around from the speaker.

That dumb Buddy! That dumb, dumb Buddy! "Hurry," she hissed at him, and darted away from the house. They raced across the lawn for the cluster of bushes near the gate. Out of breath, they flopped down behind it just as Von Desch came around the back corner of the house. He looked in all directions, then walked to the front path. Leslie wished she hadn't come and hoped they wouldn't have to hide long. She had to get home before Mama did.

Von Desch stood still for a moment. Then the sound of laughter came from the street. As Von Desch hurried to the gate, Leslie held her breath. He had to pass close to her and Buddy.

Now he spoke to two boys who were pushing at each other near the curb. "Hey, vere you boys chust sneaking around my blace?"

"No, we wouldn't go near your rotten place," one said boldly. The other giggled.

Von Desch muttered something Leslie couldn't catch, then turned and went to the back corner of the house. There he halted, peering around, his head lifted like a bird dog sniffing the wind.

Buddy got to his feet. "Run," he yelled to Leslie.

Von Desch turned swiftly at the sound and started toward them.

Oh, that dumb, dumb Buddy. They could have hidden until Von Desch had gone inside. Now he was coming at them full speed. She jumped up and raced for the gate.

Buddy tripped, stumbled, and fell full length on the grass. In an instant, Von Desch was upon him, yanking him to his feet. Leslie kept on going. At the gate, she could hear them struggling and Buddy yelling, "Let me go." She stopped and looked back. Von Desch was pulling Buddy along with one hand on Buddy's arm and the other on his collar.

Leslie started through the gate and stopped. She couldn't run off and leave Buddy at the mercy of Von Desch. Wishing she had listened to Mama instead of meddling, she turned back. And what would Papa think? Why did she ever go along with Buddy in the first place?

She caught up with them as Von Desch was trying to push Buddy through the back door. Holding tightly to the door frame, Buddy was struggling to free himself.

"Let me go," he screeched, panting and wide-eyed.

Leslie ran up to them. Von Desch turned to her. "You, too, get in here at vonce." His accent was heavy.

"No, I won't," she said, gasping, "and you let him go." She grabbed Buddy's jacket and pulled hard. But that only weakened Buddy's hold on the door frame, and before either could escape, Von Desch had shoved Buddy through the doorway and Leslie after him.

Right inside there were two stairways. One led down into the dim cellar, and the other—a short one of five steps—led up to the kitchen. Von Desch pushed both of them toward the cellar steps so roughly that they almost fell down headfirst. He came right behind them and shoved them past the big round furnace to the front of the cellar, which was the full length of the house.

They passed one small curtained-off space. Above the heavy curtains, Leslie could see the broken window they had peeked through from outside.

"Sit," Von Desch ordered at the far end of the cellar. "Sit on ze floor."

She and Buddy lowered themselves slowly. The floor was dusty and littered with old curled wood shavings. In the dimness, she could see Buddy's sweaty, pale face and knew she must look the same. She wondered suddenly where Mrs. Von Desch was. She must be out somewhere, or else she would have investigated the disturbance.

"Now stay," ordered Von Desch. He began to rummage through a stack of odds and ends on a worktable in the corner. Not seeming to find what he wanted, he looked back at them and barked, "Stay," again, then went toward the stairs.

He had scarcely gotten halfway up before Leslie rose. Buddy clambered to his feet beside her. "I'm scared," he whispered.

"So am I." She wondered what Von Desch intended to do with them. Maybe there were gestapo agents in Emmetsville, too, and Von Desch would hand her and Buddy over to them. But she shouldn't think that way. They had to get out of there.

"Come on." She led the way back to the stairs, and they crouched in the space underneath. Since the steps had no backs, she could see through them. Again, she glimpsed the curtained-off part.

Leslie realized they still couldn't be sure Von Desch was a Nazi. If they did get out and report him, what would be found? He could even have her and Buddy arrested for trespassing. They *were* trespassing—he hadn't asked them to come here. She shivered at the thought and twisted a strand of her hair into a tight string.

From upstairs came sounds of Von Desch moving about.

"If he comes down again," Leslie told Buddy, pointing, "and goes back there to look for us, we have to get out fast."

"I'm scared," Buddy whispered again.

"So am I, but when I poke you, run like the devil up the stairs. And," she added, "don't stumble."

They were squatting amid leftover pieces of wood and short lengths of old, corroded pipe.

Suddenly Von Desch was at the head of the stairs. Leslie held her breath and pressed her sweaty palms together. The sound of his thumping down the steps terrified her. When he reached the last one, Leslie could see a piece of thin rope dangling from his hand. A rope! Was he going to hang them? But that would be murder. Maybe he was going to tie them up and leave them there to starve. There was no way she would wait for that.

But Von Desch dropped the skinny rope in front of

the heavy curtains. Maybe he was going to use it to pack up his equipment. Maybe he was going to leave town soon.

"Nobody else out zere," he muttered. He must have been checking up. "Now I vant to know vy you vere sneaking around," he said loudly as he went back to where he had left them.

Leslie quickly crawled out from under the stairs, pulling Buddy after her.

She gave Buddy a vicious poke. He hesitated and she poked him again. "Go," she hissed. He lurched forward and scrambled up the steps, sounding like a herd of buffalo.

Von Desch came bounding back. Before he could reach the bottom step, Leslie lowered her head and ran straight at him like a billy goat. She butted him hard in the stomach. As he flew backward, he crashed into some old crates and sprawled on the floor.

Leslie sped up the steps, her heart pounding as though it would fly right out of her body. She couldn't make her feet go quickly enough, and her breath came short and fast. As she slammed through the door, she heard Von Desch struggling after her.

"I show you to trespass on my broperty, svine," he was shouting at them.

Buddy, white-faced, stood waiting for her on the lawn.

"Come on," she shrieked, racing past him across the grass. Buddy followed, but when she looked back at him, he stumbled briefly.

"Don't fall," she warned him. "I'm not going back for you again."

Von Desch was already tearing after them, but they reached the gate and hurtled through it to the sidewalk before he could catch up. They kept running until they came to the end of his hedge and then stopped.

"Rotten creep," Leslie stammered between gasps.

"Yeah, rotten lousy creep." Buddy was panting like a dog after a rabbit chase. "Now do you believe me?"

"Buddy, we don't *know* that he's a Nazi."

"I guess we don't," Buddy answered. Then he hung his head. "Leslie?"

"Yeah?"

"You won't tell anybody I was so—so scared, will you?"

Poor Buddy—at a time like this he worries about not looking important. "Good gosh, no. I'm not even going to tell anybody I was here." Buddy breathed loudly in relief. "But if *you're* going to tell anybody you were here," she continued, "don't tell them I was with you." She wanted time to think of what she would do next.

"I won't," Buddy promised.

"Maybe," Leslie went on, "Von Desch won't do

anything about our trespassing if we don't make trouble for him." She hoped he wouldn't try to get back at them in any way.

"Yeah," Buddy agreed, "maybe he'll forget all about it."

Leslie sure was glad Kenny wasn't with her now. "We'd better hurry," she told Buddy. But she was surprised when she looked up at the sky. According to the sun, only a short time had passed since she and Buddy had sneaked onto Von Desch's lawn. When they were in the cellar, it seemed as if they'd been there a million years.

What had Von Desch intended to do to them? she wondered. What could he do except hand them over to the police or their parents? But if he was guilty of something himself, he couldn't report them without being found out. Maybe he was just trying to scare them so that they'd stay away from his place.

7

As they started up the street, the wind grew stronger and dark clouds began to gather in the western sky. "I'm not going to tell anybody I was here," Leslie repeated. That meant Mama and Kenny and Ruthie.

"Me, neither. We didn't find out anything, anyhow."

"Maybe it's just as well," Leslie said, but the word *oferdon* rang in the back of her mind. She looked at the sky. "It's really clouding up. And the wind is getting strong. I have to hurry. So long." She ran for home as fast as she could, leaving Buddy to lumber along alone.

Shortly after she reached the house, Kenny came in. Thank goodness, she didn't have to go after him.

By the time Mama came home, the wind was whipping high and hard through the top of the elm tree out front.

"I believe we should go pell-mell for the groceries

before supper," Mama said, "so we can miss the storm."

"But I'm hungry," Kenny said.

"Have an apple," Mama told him. "We'll eat as soon as we get back."

She ran a comb through her hair quickly and reddened her lips. Frowning at her lipstick, she murmured, "I can't get used to cardboard tubes." She fumbled as she tried to fit the cap back on the frayed edge.

Leslie was tired of being reminded that most of the metal obtainable was used for tanks and planes. Then she thought of Papa and felt guilty.

The rain held off, but the wind was still strong when they came out of the grocery market. Clouds were churning low overhead, and sheet lightning flared on the horizon.

"It's pretty late in the season for thunderstorms," Mama said. "I wonder if we could still get out to Zimmerman's before the rain starts."

Mama liked farm-fresh eggs. "I hope his apples are reasonable, too." Mama had known the Zimmerman family a long time. Mr. Zimmerman was a widower now, but he and his younger son, Leonard, still ran the small farm. His older son, Walter, was overseas.

Leslie liked the extra ride—six more blocks to the

edge of town. "I don't think we'll get caught in the rain," she told Mama. She wished she could also tell Mama about going to Von Desch's place with Buddy and getting caught, but Mama would be furious to know she had been meddling like that. Yet, if Von Desch was doing something un-American, he should be reported. Well, she couldn't worry about that now.

As they neared the farm, the first thing Leslie saw was the old, round, unused water tower in the field beside the farmhouse. She had seen it a hundred times before but never thought a thing of it. Now excitement raced through her. She could picture a huge flag painted on it. It would be better than a billboard.

Mr. Zimmerman nodded silently as Leonard helped him wait on Mama. Within a few minutes, Mama was paying for her purchases. While she and Kenny put them in the car, Leslie hung back and asked Mr. Zimmerman, "Who owns the water tower?"

"I do. It came with the farm. There was a windmill, too, but it's long gone." He didn't look at her but away out to the horizon. Then he turned toward the house.

Leslie stepped after him. "Is it safe?" She knew lots of things just rotted away when they weren't used anymore.

"Yes, it's safe. It's a landmark. I keep it in repair."

He stared at her. His words were curt. "But why are you bothering me about this now?"

"Could I paint a big flag on it?" She hadn't meant to be so blunt, but she couldn't wait any longer to ask.

Mr. Zimmerman stopped and turned. "No." His voice was loud and firm. "No, I don't want any flag up there."

Leslie backed off. What in the world was wrong with Mr. Zimmerman? Why was he so different—so snappish? She could only stare after him.

As he moved away, Leonard came over to her. "Don't feel hurt, Leslie," he said. "My father is all broken up. We just got word today. Walter was killed in action in New Guinea."

"Oh, I'm sorry, I'm sorry." She ran to the car and slid into the front seat.

Mama was looking squarely at her. "What was that all about?" Mama asked.

"Walter was killed."

"Mr. Zimmerman's Walter?"

Leslie nodded, squeezing her hands together tightly.

"Oh, dear God," Mama said softly. "No wonder he was so—so distant and quiet."

"I never told him why I wanted the flag."

Mama turned the ignition key. "The flag?"

"Yes," Leslie answered. "I asked him if we could have a flag painted on the tower. I wanted it for Papa when he comes home."

Mama shook her head slowly. "It would remind the poor man of Walter, I guess."

Kenny leaned over from the back seat, letting out a loud sigh. "Poor Walter." Then, as though he'd forgotten about Walter that fast, he added, "We could try for a garage again for the flag."

"I guess that's all we can do," Leslie said. "Just don't tell any of the kids, not even Tony. It has to be a surprise."

Kenny said, "Okay," and settled back.

"That's what my essay was about," Leslie said, thinking—"and now that idea is already falling apart." Then she told Mama of the other essays and of what Miss Ellinger had said about marching in the Armistice Day parade. "Why don't you get a uniform and march with the AWVS, Mama?"

"Because a uniform costs thirty dollars. I can think of better ways to spend that much money."

"Well, you belong to them. Couldn't you just wear your regular clothes? You did enough work for them to march with them."

"I guess I could if I wanted to. I just never asked. Now we better hurry or we'll get caught in the rain."

They made it home just as the first drops started to fall. Mama pulled up to the curb at the point nearest to the front door. They each grabbed a bag and raced for the house.

"I'll just leave the car there overnight," Mama said as they were all drying off inside. Then she started supper.

Mama peeked out once at the car. "I guess one night on the street won't hurt it," she said.

Leslie scarcely heard her. What a day this had been. She would be glad to go to bed, go to sleep, and forget it.

But tomorrow was Saturday. She hoped the rain would stop, because if the papers got wet on the way to the collection center, they couldn't be counted. They would weigh more, and that would be cheating.

In the middle of the night, Leslie awakened. The rain was dashing against her window. Before she could fall back to sleep, she began to think of Von Desch and of *oferdon*. If he'd been talking about Overton Steel, she was sure the police ought to know. But if she was wrong, she might hurt him and his wife. Still, she felt someone should be told. Besides, Von Desch hadn't cared about her and Buddy when they were in his cellar.

By morning the rain had stopped. The sky was still gray and cloudy, and little puddles lingered in the backyard and in broken places in the street.

Mama worked only a half day on Saturday. She left Leslie a note: "If you wait until I get home, I'll drive you to the collection center."

Leslie was too impatient to wait. "We could start, and if it rains, we'll stop until Mama gets home," she told Kenny.

Kenny nodded and went on with his breakfast.

Leslie finished hers in a hurry. "Come on," she said. "If we hurry, we can beat the rain."

They piled the papers on the old express wagon. It would take several trips. "Don't you tell any of the kids about the flag," she reminded Kenny when they started out. She was glad Kenny didn't know about her going to Von Desch's place with Buddy.

On their last trip, they had fewer bundles of papers. They put the bags of cans on top. Leslie pulled the wagon, and Kenny carried the jar of grease in a brown paper bag. Then he saw Tony and walked with him.

Halfway to the center, Leslie met Buddy and some other kids. Buddy was lagging behind, lugging two bundles of papers in his arms. "Let me put mine on top of yours," he suggested, "and I'll pull the wagon."

"Okay," Leslie agreed, lifting the bags of cans—

they weren't hard to carry. "But be careful." She didn't fully trust Buddy with anything.

She hoped he had forgotten about yesterday afternoon. No such luck. He came close to her with a know-something grin and half whispered, "I was right about old Von Desch and his shortwave radio, wasn't I?"

She nodded. Buddy didn't seem scared anymore.

"Well, do you think we ought to report him?" he asked.

Hearing him say what she had thought sort of startled Leslie. "I was thinking of that, too, but we can't prove anything. I guess we'd best forget the whole thing." No matter what she decided to do, she wasn't sure she wanted Buddy in on it with her. Yet he had told her about Von Desch. . . .

His smirk lessened and he shrugged. "Yeah, I guess so. Who knows what he was saying, anyhow?"

"I'd hate for him to report us for trespassing," Leslie added. "I'd hate to have to explain that to anybody."

Buddy wagged his head. "Me, too."

Suddenly Leslie heard someone screaming her name. "Leslie, Leslie."

It was Kenny.

"Be careful," she told Buddy, and headed back toward Kenny. He was almost crying. At his feet lay a brown paper bag oozing an oily liquid.

"Tony stumbled and bumped into me." He pointed downward. "I dropped the grease." Tony stood by, silent.

"Okay, okay," Leslie said soothingly. "But we can't let it lie there." All they needed was for someone to get cut on the glass. She handed him the bags of cans and looked around.

Spotting a trash container at the corner, she gathered up the greasy mess. Just as she was dropping it in, her eye caught Buddy bumping the wagon down off the curb. It tipped over, and when the top bundles of papers landed in the wet gutter, the cord broke. The next minute, papers were flying all over. If everybody's war effort ends like this, Leslie thought, we'll sure lose the war.

For a minute, she wished things could be the way they'd been before. They wouldn't be collecting all this junk and dragging it around town. Mama wouldn't be going out to work. Papa would be home, and she and Mary would be playing jacks on the front porch after supper or whenever they felt like it.

She helped Buddy gather up the papers. They were sloppy from the wet spots in the street. What was left of the bundles was drenched from the water in the gutter.

"I told you to be careful," she hissed at Buddy.

"So I'm a dummkopf."

Leslie knew he got that from the Nazis in the war movies.

When they reached the center on the lot behind the library, other people's deposits were already piled high. Going to the corner where two fathers had volunteered to oversee their school's collections, they turned in the rest of the papers and cans, and left.

8

Mama was home from work when they got there. After they all had some lunch, she said, "I guess I might as well put the car in the driveway. I don't want it on the street all day." She paused a moment. "And don't forget, I'm on duty at the station from three till four-thirty."

Mama would stand behind the red, white, and blue counter at the railroad depot and serve coffee and doughnuts to the servicemen. And she'd give directions to anyone who needed them.

"Can we go along?" Kenny asked. He loved to meet the servicemen.

"Sure, you may always go with me, as long as you behave," Mama answered. Then she went out to the car. Almost immediately she came back in, looking very disturbed.

"The car won't start," she said.

"Why?" Kenny asked.

"I have no idea." She turned to go outside again.

Leslie and Kenny followed. She turned the ignition key. No response. She turned it again and again. Not even a sputter.

Leslie glanced at the gas gauge. "Maybe we're out of gas, Mama."

"We couldn't be. We had plenty left last evening." Mama peered at the gauge. "But it says empty."

"I'll bet it was siphoned," Kenny said, hanging over the back of the seat. He made motions of putting one end of a tube into the gas tank and the other into his mouth. Then he pulled in his breath with a loud sucking sound. "Tony's father's car was siphoned."

Leslie had heard of gas being siphoned but never thought it would happen to them.

"Whoever would do such a thing?" Mama murmured. "And right out on the street."

But the streetlight was four doors away from their house. And the big elm on the tree bank kept the light from reaching their place.

Mama's hands were gripping the steering wheel tightly. "I was depending on what we had in the tank and my last coupon to have enough gas to go to Grandma's when Papa comes home."

They all slid slowly out of the car. Mama went to the trunk, and, opening it, took out a battered five-gallon can. A withered potato served as a cork.

"Get the wagon and go to the service station,"

Mama said. "I'll get the gas coupon and money for you. I hope nothing else is wrong with the car."

One coupon was worth four gallons.

Kenny went along with Leslie and insisted on pulling the wagon.

"All right," she told him, "but be careful—not like that Buddy."

"Okay, okay."

They waved to Mama and hurried off. At the station, they gave the can to the attendant.

"I think we were siphoned," Kenny blurted out.

"Not again!" The attendant wagged his head. "You're the fourth one around here. I wish we could catch that crook."

"So do I," Leslie said, "and give him to Hitler." Then, brushing her hair back from her forehead, she asked right out, "How can we get emergency gas?"

"Well, you have to go to the ration board," the attendant told her. "Maybe they'll give you extra coupons—if your reason is good enough."

"My father's coming home on leave," Leslie said. And that was a good enough reason for her, but probably not for the board.

Going home, she and Kenny were very careful, especially at the curbs. They were very careful, too, when they helped Mama put the gas into the car tank.

Boy, what a world! Leslie thought. There was Papa off in the service and he couldn't even see his own mother when he was home on leave! Well, no matter what, she was going to get gas. Papa was going to have his flag and gas for the car, too. And she was going to help Mama get stockings. They deserved what they needed just as much as anyone else, she thought angrily. They were doing all they could for the war effort.

As always, she wished she could do something herself to make a difference. Her thoughts turned to Von Desch. If he *was* a Nazi, he should be reported just in case whatever he was doing was hurting the country. Perhaps she should tell Buddy to report him, but she was afraid Buddy would botch things. If she called the police herself and didn't give her name, no one would know who called. That would be about the best way, she figured. She decided, then, that the first chance she got, she would phone the police.

Mama's stint at the station proved so dull that Leslie wished she had stayed home. Two trains came in with no servicemen on board. As the second one was about to pull out, two sailors dashed into the station, grabbed doughnuts and coffee, and jumped aboard.

"Couldn't even talk to them," Kenny complained.

On the way home, they met Mary. She was just

coming back from the collection center. Mama and Kenny walked on, and Leslie hung back to walk with Mary.

"I didn't take my stuff in until three o'clock. Then I stayed till they told who won," Mary explained. "Our room won the can pennant."

"Good," Leslie said, but she didn't feel overly excited. Just as she'd guessed, they'd missed the paper pennant by a few pounds. She was sure Buddy's carelessness had caused their loss. The stolen gas also helped to dampen her spirits. She was about to mention it when Mary grinned widely.

"Guess what? I got an answer from my brother— my first V-mail letter." Mary's brother was in the army overseas. "It's just like a picture."

"Great. I want to see it," Leslie said. She remembered when Mary wrote a V-mail letter to her brother on a form sheet that you folded in on its four sides to make it into an envelope. Mama would probably get V-mail from Papa when he went overseas.

They reached Mary's corner. "Well, here's where I turn," Mary said. "I'll bring my letter to school on Monday. Bye."

On Monday morning, just before she left for school, Leslie thought of her decision to call the police. If she was going to do anything about Von Desch, she had to do it right now. But she didn't want Kenny to hear her make the call.

"I forgot something," she said at the door. "Go ahead, but wait for me at the corner."

Kenny nodded. As soon as the door closed behind him, Leslie had doubts again. But she wasn't going to back out now. She only wished she could tell the police that Von Desch had caught her and Buddy. They had been trespassing, though, and they could not prove that Von Desch was a Nazi spy. Besides, Mama would have a fit if she knew what Leslie had been up to.

Leslie rehearsed what she'd say—she'd have to get it out all at once so she wouldn't forget anything—and picked up the receiver. Please don't let me hurt anyone, she begged silently.

When a voice said, "Sergeant Abe Jackson," she nearly lost her nerve. Then she plunged in.

"I want to report a man who might be a Nazi spy. His name is Oscar Von Desch and he lives on Laramie Street. He has a shortwave radio and he talked about Overton Steel Company." She stopped. The last part might not be true. She could have bitten her tongue for saying it.

"Yes, I got all that," Sergeant Jackson said. "Who's calling?"

Leslie hung up. Her hand was shaking. She almost

wished she hadn't called, but it was done. Then she was glad she had. Boy, was she mixed up! Now there was nothing to do but wait to see what came of it. If her call proved to be a good thing, she'd make sure Buddy got his share of the credit. She didn't doubt, though, that he'd make sure of that himself.

But what if, instead of helping the war effort, she had hurt someone? She mustn't think that way. If it was right to report suspicious things, she had only done her duty.

Snatching up her books, she hurried out to the corner. When she saw Kenny, some of the confused feeling left her, and by the time they'd reached school, she had calmed down. No one knew she'd made the call, she assured herself.

She was tired of thinking of Von Desch. She wanted to think of Papa's flag and find a place for it. That was the most important thing, no matter what. Then there was the problem of getting extra gas for the car.

At the school door, Mary came over to her. "You're late," Mary said. "You'll have to wait till lunchtime to see my letter."

When Mary showed it to her at the lunch table, Buddy reached across for it. Mary quickly jammed it into her pocket.

"So keep it," Buddy said. "I'll get one from my

father when he goes overseas." He went on with his lunch.

Then Leslie said, "I have some lousy news. Someone stole the gas out of our car."

"Oh, that's awful," Mary said, unwrapping a sandwich.

Again, Buddy leaned forward. "Your car got siphoned? That's tough." He and some of the boys began imitating a car that wouldn't start.

Creeps, Leslie thought, and turned away from them. It seemed Buddy had forgotten all about Von Desch.

After school, Buddy ran clumsily after her and Mary. The sole of one of his shoes was loose and made a slap-slap sound. "Maybe I can help you get gas for your car," he said.

"How?" Mary giggled. "Are you going to dig an oil well?"

"Oooh, smart!" Buddy pointed to his forehead.

Mary laughed. "See you," she said to Leslie, and turned the corner.

Just then Kenny, who'd been lagging behind, came abreast of them. Buddy was telling Leslie, "I'll give you a gas coupon for a shoe coupon."

"My shoe coupon?" Buddy certainly had his nerve.

"Sure. Do something for your country."

"My country? You'll get the shoes."

"Well." Buddy looked at his feet. "Mine wear out faster than yours."

Leslie was about to tell him that if he didn't walk like a horse his shoes would last longer, but she didn't. She didn't want to make him mad. She wanted a gas coupon for Papa.

"Well, okay," she said slowly.

"And how about you, Kenny?" Buddy asked. "I'll give you a gas coupon, too, for your shoe coupon."

"Okay." Kenny's grin came and went.

This is too much, Leslie thought, and protested. "What if we need shoes?"

Buddy put up his hand. "Don't worry. Pete down at Benjamin's will sell you sneakers without a coupon. The soles are reclaimed rubber."

Before she could ask why he didn't get sneakers himself, Buddy informed her. "I wear them out too fast. I have to have leather shoes."

Then he waved them forward. "Come on. I'll get my coupons and bring them right over to your house."

Leslie nodded. Looking at Buddy, she wondered what he would say if she told him she'd phoned the police about Von Desch. She quickly put the thought out of her mind. She had to concentrate on the gas coupons now.

By the time she and Kenny had reached home, Leslie was having second thoughts about giving up their shoe coupons. But ten minutes later, when she saw the two gas coupons Buddy had brought to the door, she went through with the trade.

After Buddy left, Kenny asked, "What shall we tell Mama?" His eyes looked worried.

"The truth," Leslie answered, twisting a strand of hair. She was feeling a little worried herself. "I'm sure she'll be glad to get the gas coupons."

As soon as Mama came through the door from work, they showed them to her. She was very pleased, until they told her what they had traded.

Mama frowned. "Now neither of you can get a pair of shoes until the new coupons are issued."

Leslie knew this and hoped hers would last. But she tried to be matter-of-fact. "Buddy needs them more than we do. He wears shoes out fast."

"Yeah." Kenny chuckled. "He walks like a horse."

Leslie agreed. "He sure does—like he has four feet, two in each shoe."

Kenny laughed loudly and went around the room stomping his feet down hard. Clomp, clomp, clomp.

"That will be enough of that," Mama said. Then her voice softened. "I'm glad you got the gas coupons, but you should have asked me first, so that I could have looked into the matter." She took off her coat.

Just then the doorbell rang. "Now what?" Mama's voice was annoyed again, and she looked tired and nervous. "Who could that be?" Taking a deep breath, she squared her shoulders.

"I'll see." Kenny rushed to the front door. When he opened it, he stood silently, stiff as a statue.

Right behind him, Leslie peered over his shoulder and saw a woman. It was Buddy's mother. I'll bet she needs the gas coupons and wants them back, Leslie told herself. She stammered, "C-come in."

"Is your mother home?"

"Y-yes," Leslie answered, and called, "Mama, Mrs. Haver wants to see you."

Still holding her coat, Mama came into the hallway.

"Hello," Buddy's mother said, "I hope I'm not catching you at a bad time." Her tone was warm.

"No, no," Mama said, shifting her coat from one arm to the other.

"Well," Buddy's mother went on. "I brought one of the shoe coupons back. One coupon for Buddy is worth two for gas."

"How nice of you." Mama was openly relieved. "But won't you need gas for your car, too?"

"No, our car is finished. It needs a new carburetor, among other things. It's just sitting there since my husband left."

"That's very kind of you. Won't you have a chair? I'll get some coffee."

"No, thank you. I'm in a hurry. I must get supper ready. Bye, now."

Closing the door softly behind the woman, Mama said, "We have one shoe coupon and two for gas." She smiled, and her whole face shone.

Leslie sighed. Sometimes, she thought, Buddy does something worthwhile, even if he isn't trying too hard.

"But," Mama was saying, "not a word about this to Papa. He would only worry."

Leslie agreed. Kenny nodded vigorously.

Papa would probably worry more, Leslie thought, if he knew she'd tried to turn in Oscar Von Desch. Her feelings were getting all mixed up again. She hoped the police would think it was just a crank call and not even investigate. Better still, she hoped they had forgotten all about it by now.

9

The first thing Leslie thought when she awoke the following morning was that Papa would be home the weekend after next. She had scarcely finished the thought before she hopped out of bed with excitement racing through her.

She grabbed a purple jumper and lavender blouse from her closet, gave her face a quick splash in the bathroom, brushed her teeth, and ran a comb through her hair. Then she stopped short, her thoughts clouding. This was Tuesday. Mama had told her last night, "Don't forget, Benjamin's might get some hosiery in. You will go there directly from school."

"Yes, Mama," she had promised.

When she and Kenny reached Benjamin's that afternoon, Leslie heard the saleslady tell a customer, "No, the only hosiery left is cotton lisle."

Cotton lisle—Mama wore them to work sometimes, but she would want more sheer stockings for dress-up. "Come on," Leslie told Kenny, "they don't have any."

"Good," Kenny said, "we don't have to wait."

In a way, Leslie was relieved, too, but she felt sorry that Mama would be disappointed again.

On the way home, they searched for garages that might have a nice wall for a flag. Leslie thought two of them would do, but the owners weren't in love with her idea.

The next day was no better. On Thursday afternoon, Leslie made up her mind—she would try for the tower again. Setting her books on the dining room table, she asked Kenny, "Do you want to go to Mr. Zimmerman's with me? I'm going to ask him again to use the water tower for my flag."

Kenny shook his head. "I'm tired. I don't feel like walking all the way down there. He'll say no, anyhow."

Leslie felt the same way, but she had to try. "Well, do you want to call Tony and see if you can go to his place?"

"Sure."

In a few short moments, Kenny returned. "He says okay."

"All right, but don't go anyplace else—and don't tell him about the flag."

She met Mr. Zimmerman coming out of the barn. "I'm terribly sorry about Walter," she told him.

He nodded. "Thank you," he said, but he kept going toward the house.

Leslie fell into step with him and began, "I'd like— I'd like to tell you why we wanted a flag on the tower."

Mr. Zimmerman stopped and looked straight at her. If he says no again, she thought, I'm sunk. Quickly, she continued, "It will honor all the servicemen, and my father is coming home Sunday after next."

Mr. Zimmerman's face softened. Leslie could see tears at the corners of his eyes. "I—I guess I would— I'd be honoring them, too." He faltered. "In a way."

Leslie twisted a strand of hair into a tight string. "Oh, yes. Yes, you would."

Mr. Zimmerman nodded again. "Go ahead if you want to." He looked up at the tower and took a deep breath. "It will be a good place for a flag."

"Oh, thank you, thank you." Leslie wished she could hug him. Then an idea spun into her mind. "It will honor Walter in a special way, I promise."

Suddenly she remembered the billboard and that it cost to use the space on one. Would the tower space cost, too? "Would there be a charge for using it?" she asked.

"No, no charge." For a moment, Mr. Zimmerman looked puzzled. "But who is going to do this?"

"Our schoolteacher said some volunteers might do it."

Mr. Zimmerman looked up at the tower. "Leonard and I could help, but"—he hesitated—"but we couldn't draw or sketch a flag. Maybe Walter could've. He was good at drawing." His face crumpled.

Leslie had to look away. "A man at the Outdoor Advertising Company said he'd help," she said. "I think he could draw it." At least she hoped Dave could.

Once more Mr. Zimmerman nodded, and went on to the house.

Leslie ran all the way home. Kenny was half lying, half sitting on the sofa when she burst in, panting for breath.

"I got it! I got it!"

"What?"

"The tower! Mr. Zimmerman said we could use it for the flag."

"That's great." Kenny sat straight up.

Leslie dashed for the phone. "I have to call Dave right away and see when he can start." She took the Outdoor Advertising Company number from her notebook and dialed. She heard someone say hello, and asked for Dave.

"I'm sorry," a lady's voice said, "but he's not here."

"Oh." Leslie could feel her shoulders droop.

"But he does drop by sometimes on the way home from work," the lady added. "And he always starts from here in the morning. Could I give him a message?"

Leslie felt a little better. "Y-yes. Could you tell him Leslie called? Tell him I have a place for the flag."

"Flag?"

"Yes, he knows about it, and tell him to please call me at my house." She gave the number.

"Very well. I'll do that."

"Thank you." Leslie hung up, but she felt let down. She'd probably have to wait till tomorrow morning. But I have the tower, she told herself.

Mama was happy for Leslie. "That's fine. I hope Mr. Zimmerman won't hurt too much, being reminded of Walter by the flag."

"No, he knows we'll honor Walter, too."

Just then the phone rang. Mama was closest to it. "I'll get it." After a moment, she turned to Leslie, her brows drawing together. "Someone named Dave. Who's that?"

"The—the billboard man," Leslie sputtered, reaching for the phone. "He said he'd paint the flag for us."

"Hello. This is Leslie."

"Hi. Dave here. Got your message."

"Yes, we can paint the flag on the water tower on Zimmerman's farm. Mr. Zimmerman said we could."

"Fine, fine. I know where that is," Dave said. "I have some time off next week, so I can easily do it. I can use some of the company equipment."

"But can you," Leslie started—she had better ask right away—"can you draw? Mr. Zimmerman said he'd help, but he can't draw a flag."

"Sketching's a hobby of mine," Dave answered. "I went to art school before I joined the navy. No problem." After a slight pause, he added, "Tomorrow's Friday—maybe I'll get over there to make a rough drawing tomorrow evening."

"That's great. I'll call Mr. Zimmerman and tell him you're coming." She hung up.

Mama stood close by, smiling. "Well, you sure are a go-getter, Leslie. Don't forget to offer to pay for the paint. You'll have to think of a way to get the money."

Leslie nodded. She had thought of the cost, but she had hoped that problem would work itself out. She had to agree with Mama, though—the responsibility should be hers. She called Mr. Zimmerman and told him Dave would sketch the flag.

The next morning, before class, she told Miss Ellinger her good news.

"On a water tower," Miss Ellinger said, clasping

her hands together. "That's a marvelous idea." She lowered her voice. "But we'll still keep it quiet so that no boys will be running out there to help."

"Yes." Leslie could see what Miss Ellinger meant. If it were strictly a classroom project, all the pupils could take part in it. Since it wasn't, it would be better to keep the other kids out of it. Dave and his helpers probably wouldn't want to be pestered by the boys.

At lunchtime, Leslie wanted to chat with Mary about the flag, but Buddy and some boys were sitting too close. Instead, on the way out, she whispered her news to Mary. "But," she ended, "don't tell anyone."

Mary promised, crossing her heart.

After school, she couldn't wait. "Let's leave our books at home," she told Kenny, "and go see the water tower."

Kenny needed no coaxing. "I like Dave," he said. So, dropping their books inside their door, they hurried off again.

"If you see Tony on the way, or any of the other kids, don't tell them where we're going," she warned Kenny. "It has to be a secret. Mary's the only other one who knows."

Kenny nodded. "I won't tell."

The eight blocks seemed much farther to Leslie today. Her feet couldn't go fast enough. When they reached the farm, she looked at the tower immediately. There, on the side toward the road, was the outline of a huge flag. It wasn't made of just straight lines. Only the drawing of the pole was straight; the lines of the flag were curved as though the flag were snapping in the wind. The lines were faint, and she guessed people couldn't see the flag unless they were looking for it. But, oh, it was going to be a glorious flag.

There was a sort of platform around the tower and ladders high enough to reach it, but no workers were there.

"How do you like it?" a man's voice asked.

Leslie started and turned to see Dave coming toward them. Then she saw the truck near the barn.

"It's great," she said. "But I didn't think you'd have started it yet."

"I was through with work at noon and came right over."

"It sure is neat," Kenny said.

"Well"—Dave rubbed his jaw—"the painting won't take long. Not with the Zimmermans helping, and another friend of mine."

"Will it be done by next Saturday?" Leslie was anxious.

"If the weather holds up," Dave told her. "And I believe it will. Will your father be home by then?"

"He's supposed to come early the next morning."

"Fine. I hope he likes it. Maybe I'll get a chance to meet him."

"I know he'll like it," Leslie said. "And he'll be glad to meet you."

"For sure he will," Kenny added. Then he ran off to play with Rex, the old farm dog.

Leslie looked around to see that no one could hear. Then she asked Dave about her special honor for Walter—an extra star in gold. "Could you do it the very last thing so that it would be a surprise for Mr. Zimmerman?"

"Sure thing," Dave assured her.

Knowing the other question she had to ask Dave, Leslie shifted her feet and clasped her hands tightly. "I guess we should pay for the paint. How much will it be?" She didn't know yet exactly where she would get the money.

"Oh, I have some white—I do house painting, too. And the Zimmermans have some red from their barn. And my friend is chipping in. I'm not sure, but maybe we'll have enough."

"Well, if you have to buy more, my mother said we'd take care of it." She knew that was stretching the truth.

"Fine." Dave gave them a little salute and went back to his truck.

As they walked home, Leslie told Kenny. "We might have to pay for some of the paint."

"How?"

"We'll have to earn the money."

"How?"

"I could baby-sit and you could do yard work," Leslie said.

"Okay." Kenny smiled.

For some reason, Leslie thought, it sounded easy.

At home, Leslie went upstairs for her dime bank, a silver-colored tube with a slot to slide dimes into. It reminded her of the change holders the trolley conductor wore on a belt in front of his stomach. It could hold five dollars' worth of dimes. She unscrewed the top and shook out the coins.

"I have sixty cents," she said. "How much do you have?"

"Thirty cents."

"That's not enough for a can of paint." Leslie paused. "We'd better find some jobs. I'm going to see Mrs. Keller. She let me mind Willie once in July."

"Can I come along?"

"Okay, but behave."

Kenny nodded.

When they reached the Keller house, Mrs. Keller was carrying her baby across the sidewalk toward the car. Four-year-old Willie was clutching her skirt and crying.

"Is something wrong?" Leslie asked.

"I have to take the baby to the doctor for his checkup and we're late."

"I'll sit with Willie for twenty-five cents—if you want me to." Immediately Leslie felt greedy, mentioning money when Mrs. Keller was in a hurry.

"Fine. Then I won't have to take him along. He's been beastly all day. Willie, stay with Leslie. Here's the front door key."

Willie cried louder as his mother placed the baby in the canvas car seat and got in.

Kenny took Willie's hand. "Come on, Willie. I'll play with you."

Inside the house, Kenny rolled a big, bright ball to Willie, and Willie's tears stopped quickly. Then Leslie read his picture books to him and gave him some milk and a cracker. He was asleep on the sofa when his mother came home. She'd been gone only about an hour.

Mrs. Keller looked tired. "Baby is doing fine," she said as she laid the baby in his bassinet. "But thanks for taking Willie off my hands."

Leslie thought of her money but felt embarrassed to ask for it. Then, at the door, Mrs. Keller said, "Oh, just a minute," and fished in her purse.

Leslie closed her hand tightly around the quarter. "Thank you."

Mama was already home when they got there.

"I was baby-sitting for Mrs. Keller's Willie," Leslie explained. Then she told Mama about the progress Dave had already made at the water tower. "It's a waving flag and it looks real." She couldn't keep the excitement out of her voice.

"That's wonderful," Mama said, "but did you find out how much the paint will cost?"

Leslie told her what Dave had said. "That's why I went to Mrs. Keller's. With what we have now, I think we can buy a can of paint."

"Good," Mama said. "I'm glad you're helping out."

"Could we go for it now, before the store closes?" Kenny asked.

Mama brushed a strand of hair back from her forehead. "No, it's nearly suppertime. You can go tomorrow morning." She sighed out loud. "I wish stockings were as easy to get as paint."

"Should we try the Circle Store tomorrow?" Leslie asked.

Mama's face brightened a bit. "Yes, when you go to the hardware store for the paint, you could stop in. And don't forget to take the note."

10

The next morning, right after breakfast, Leslie and Kenny hurried off to the hardware store. Since it was Saturday, many people had come in from the farming district outside of town, and the two salesmen were kept busy. Finally Leslie got a chance to ask the price of a gallon of white paint.

She nodded as the salesman said, "One dollar a gallon." So far, so good. "Well, we can take that," she said. "And how much are the red and blue paint?"

"Thirty-nine cents a quart. But there's an older can of red here you could have for fifteen cents." He plunked it down on the counter.

"Okay, we can take that, too." After she paid for the paint, she lifted the two cans and was surprised at the weight.

Outside, Kenny reached for the bigger one. "It will make my pitching arm strong," he said. "Papa says I have to have strong arms for baseball."

At the corner, she suddenly stopped. "I almost forgot. We have to go to the Circle Store for Mama."

Kenny looked at her with a frown but said nothing. They were a short half block away. But the only stockings the store had were black rayon. Mama wouldn't want those.

"Good." Kenny sounded overjoyed.

Even though she was glad herself at not having to wait around, Kenny's one word nettled her. "No, it's not good. Mama needs stockings."

Kenny defended himself. "I mean it's good we can take this heavy paint home right away."

Just then Ruthie rounded the corner and came toward them. Exactly what I need, Leslie told herself.

"Is Aunt Jane going to paint something?" Ruthie asked.

Leslie shrugged. "Yes, something is going to be painted." Boy, what a stupid answer, but Ruthie didn't pursue it.

"Believe it or not," Ruthie exclaimed, "I needed more wool for Papa's sweater—just a little, but I had to buy a whole hank of yarn."

That sweater again! Leslie thought. "Well, I guess they won't sell just a little," she said. "Bye."

When Mama came home at noon, Leslie said, "No stockings," right off. She didn't want to keep Mama wondering.

"I guessed as much," Mama said, taking off her coat.

"We saw Ruthie," Kenny told her.

"But we didn't tell her what the paint is for," Leslie added.

Mama raised her eyebrows. "Why not?"

Leslie shrugged. "I just don't want her to know. It's a secret."

Mama seemed to understand. "All right. It's a secret." After a pause, she said, "I'm signed up for the war-stamp booth at the Rialto afternoon show. If you want to go along, you will both get ready as soon as you've finished lunch."

It was hard for Leslie to keep her mind on the movie—another one about the war in the South Pacific. Her thoughts were still all tied up with Papa's leave, with the paint and the flag. She even thought of Von Desch and wondered if anything would come of her call to the police. If nothing did, then there could be one less thing on her mind.

But at suppertime, Mama said something that made her scalp tingle. "I just remembered—it must have slipped my mind—there were police snooping around the plant and offices this morning."

"Why?" Leslie's voice didn't sound right to herself.

"Someone said there was talk of the fifth column—"

"Fifth column? What's that?" Kenny wanted to know.

"Enemy spies trying to sneak in and work in places as if they belonged there. But I'm sure the investigation won't turn up anything."

Leslie waited nervously.

"Funny thing," Mama went on, "Von Desch's name came up. I saw him a week or so ago as I was getting onto the trolley to come home from work. He got on, too. When I said hello, he just nodded and sat down with a fellow who rides the trolley every day." Frown lines appeared between her eyebrows. "I wondered why Mr. Von Desch was down that way."

"Does the other man work at your place?" Leslie asked.

"Yes, and I thought Mr. Von Desch might be trying to get a job there, too." Mama paused and then said, "I remember your saying that people thought he was a Nazi. Who told you that?"

"Buddy and the other kids were talking about it," Leslie said, but she thought, I'll bet I'm the only one who called the police. The thought made her both anxious and proud.

"How did the police find out?" Kenny asked.

Leslie held her breath.

"Someone called but didn't give a name," Mama answered.

Leslie could feel relief wash down through her whole being. But she was sure now that she had done the right thing. She couldn't tell Mama her part in it until she knew that no one innocent had been hurt by the investigation.

Ruthie came over on Sunday afternoon to show off the knitting she had done all week. "Aunt Jane, do you think Papa will like it?"

Mama nodded her head firmly. "I know he will. It's turning out real well."

Leslie remained silent.

Kenny offered Ruthie some store-bought cookies. He had just opened the box. While she nibbled on one, Ruthie looked around as if she missed something. "I don't see anything newly painted."

Getting nosy, Leslie thought. Mama had her back turned and said nothing. Neither did Kenny.

"Not yet," Leslie ventured, hoping Ruthie would go no further.

But Ruthie immediately changed the subject. "If you ever need any gray yarn," she said, "I have lots of it."

Leslie relaxed. Thank heavens Ruthie had the habit of jumping from one subject to another.

Ruthie came over on Sunday evening, too. "Just wanted to tell you, Aunt Jane," she said, "I heard at work yesterday that Benjamin's won't be getting their hosiery in on Tuesday as usual. I forgot to mention it this afternoon." She giggled. "It pays to have friends checking around for you."

"Oh, dear," Mama said. "I was hoping I might get a pair."

"Me, too," Ruthie said. "A fellow at work asked me out on Saturday evening. Let me know if you find any."

The next day, immediately after school, Leslie caught Kenny and hurried home. "Let's get the paint and take it right down to the tower."

Kenny's eyes sparkled. "I'll get the old paintbrushes, too. Maybe Dave will let us help."

At the house, Leslie changed into an old pair of slacks that were getting too short for her. Kenny got out of his school clothes, too. Then he disappeared down the cellar steps and came back with two two-inch brushes and a screwdriver to open the cans.

"Dave's a good guy," he said as they left.

"Yeah, he sure is." All Leslie hoped for now was that they wouldn't meet any of the kids they knew.

They took turns carrying each can. One time when Kenny had the smaller can, he said, "If I throw it up and down, it will be all mixed when we get there." He tossed the can into the air and almost didn't catch it.

"Stop that," Leslie snapped at him. "If it falls and hits the ground hard, it might open and spill all over.

We can stir it with the screwdriver when we get there."

But when they reached the farm, Dave wasn't there. They didn't see Mr. Zimmerman or Leonard anywhere, either.

"Let's start painting and surprise them," Kenny suggested, and headed for the ladder.

"Wait," Leslie called. She was as eager as Kenny, but she wondered if it was a wise thing to do. Still . . . "Sure, why not." She'd love to say she had helped paint the flag. "We'll take the red paint. The last stripe down is red. That will be the easiest to reach."

When they got to the top of the ladder and crawled onto the platform that ran around the tower, Leslie looked down. She immediately doubted what they were doing.

"Whew!" Kenny said. "I'd hate to fall from here."

"Well, just don't."

He pulled the brushes from his pocket. Leslie looked at them. "They're so skinny—it will take forever."

With the screwdriver, they pried the lid off the can and stirred the paint. Then they stuck their brushes into it.

Leslie made a few strokes on the last stripe. "It's pretty, but I'm glad we don't have to do the stars." She looked up at the bright blue square. Most of the stars had been painted. So had the top four stripes.

"I like to paint," Kenny said, slapping his brush hard against the wood of the tower.

They were at it only a few minutes when they heard a motor. Kenny looked around quickly. As he shifted his position, his foot bumped the can and tipped it over. The red paint poured out. Trying to grab it, Kenny lost his balance and stepped into the red pool. His shoes slippery from the paint, he slid toward the edge of the platform, where he could easily go under the railing.

"Watch out!" Leslie screamed. "You'll fall off!"

Kenny went down on his hands and knees with a loud screech.

"Stay there," Leslie warned, stepping around the paint. "I'll help you to the ladder."

But Kenny didn't reach for her hand or move toward the ladder rung. "I can't," he gasped. His eyes were wide.

Just then, she heard a shout. "What the devil do you kids think you're doing?" It was Dave. Close behind him were Mr. Zimmerman and Leonard.

"Kenny fell," Leslie called, "and he's too scared to move."

"I'll come up and get him."

In less than two minutes, Dave was looking at them

from the top of the ladder. "Come on, Kenny, back yourself over here and put your foot on the rung. Come on, now."

Slowly, Kenny inched backward until Dave could guide his feet onto the ladder. Leslie followed them down.

When they were all safely on the ground, Leslie looked at Dave. His face was set and stern. "We wanted to help," she said, knowing the excuse was lame.

"Yes, and you both could have gotten hurt." Dave didn't look at her.

Mr. Zimmerman brought some turpentine from the barn. Dave dipped a cloth into it and cleaned Kenny's hands and shoes and the knees of his pants. Leslie had a smear on her sleeve. Dave took care of that, too.

Then he stood with his hands on his hips, looking at them. "All right, now. Either you two promise to let us grown-ups do the painting, or the deal's off."

Leslie could feel a warm, stinging sensation at the back of her eyes. "We promise," she said unsteadily. After all her rushing around and planning, this had to happen. If Mama weren't working, she'd never take Kenny anywhere else the rest of her life. She swallowed hard and pointed. "We brought a can of white paint, too."

"Fine," Dave said. "With that we should have

plenty. Now you two better get on home." His eyes were friendly again, but he didn't smile.

As soon as they were out on the road, Leslie turned to Kenny. "You're a stupid—a stupid wretch." The word had a good, hateful sound. "Nothing but a wretch," she added. "You spoil everything."

Kenny sniffed and hung his head. He walked that way behind her until they were almost home. Then they passed a garden edged with clumps of dead hollyhocks. A bright cardinal sat on a swaying stalk, singing loudly. Leslie thought of Papa—Papa liked cardinals. The thought took away some of her anger. She couldn't stay mad any longer.

Glancing back at Kenny, she said, "Well, the flag will get done, anyhow."

Kenny raised his head, brightening. "Sure will," he agreed. After a moment, he asked, "Are you going to tell Mama?"

"We won't have to," Leslie said, sniffing her sleeve. "She'll smell us a mile away." But, no, she wasn't going to tell Mama the whole story. Mama had enough on her mind without worrying about two dumb kids falling off an old water tower.

As soon as they got into the house, they both darted to their rooms to change. Putting the smelly clothes into the old hamper in the cellar, Leslie said, "When the smell fades away, we'll throw them in the wash."

On her way back up the steps, she remembered that they had left the red paint and brushes and screwdriver on the platform. So what. She didn't want to think about it anymore. Papa's flag would be done, and she wasn't going to let what happened today spoil that for her.

When Mama came in from work, she wrinkled her nose. "Do I smell turpentine, or am I imagining it?"

"We were out at the tower and got some paint on us," Leslie said. "Dave took it off with turpentine."

Kenny kept silent.

Then Mama smiled. "I might have some luck at last—getting stockings, I mean. Our file girl told me Benjamin's will have hosiery on Saturday, but it probably won't arrive until almost noon. It'll be put on sale around one o'clock. If I hurry right to the store from work, I might get there in time." Mama sighed. "But you take the note and go, too. It's my last chance. I'm glad I know someone who has a friend working at the store."

Mama sighed again and went into the kitchen. Following her, Leslie got the napkins and dishes to set the table.

11

The next two days, Leslie wanted very much to see the flag, but she decided against it. "We'd better not go back too soon," she told Kenny. "I don't want Dave to get mad at us."

"That's for sure," Kenny said.

They walked partway home from school with Mary and Tony. Once, when they passed a soldier, Leslie thought of Papa. Kenny saluted and said, "Hi."

Then a car drove by with a sailor and his girl. Kenny waved to them. Farther on, near a gas station, they saw a marine and coastguardsman, talking and laughing about something. Kenny just grinned at them.

Leslie knew all the uniforms, but not the rank insignias. They all reminded her of Papa.

On Thursday evening, after shopping at the grocery market, Mama drove them to the farm for eggs. Mama was so surprised when she saw the water tower, she just sat in the car, staring at it. Her mouth opened, but no words came out. Even in the dim evening light, the flag looked bright and real. It was just about finished.

Finally Mama spoke. "Why, it's beautiful."

"And it's for Papa," Leslie said.

"It's for the other soldiers, too," Kenny reminded her.

Leslie didn't answer. In her heart, it was Papa's flag, except for the special part for Walter that she'd promised Mr. Zimmerman. But no one but she and Dave knew about the extra star.

Several times Mama told Mr. Zimmerman how lovely she thought it was.

He nodded and smiled sadly. "Just needs a touch or two more, Dave tells me," he said. "He'll be here tomorrow after lunch to finish it."

Although Mr. Zimmerman looked Leslie's way several times, he never mentioned the trouble they'd had when she and Kenny had tried to help with the painting. She could have hugged him for that.

Many people must have seen the flag by now, but no one at school had mentioned it. She was glad and remembered that none of the kids went by that way. The kids who lived around Mr. Zimmerman's farm went to Garfield School, not hers.

Friday morning, the weather was still holding up. Sunshine splashed the sidewalks and the air was mild as Leslie and Kenny walked to school. They'll finish the flag today, Leslie thought, and everything will be great—except for the war.

Then, suddenly, she noticed Mrs. Von Desch at the corner, waiting for a trolley. The woman was holding a suitcase.

"Hello, Mrs. Von Desch," Kenny said brightly.

"Hello," Leslie said, too. But Mrs. Von Desch only nodded and drew up her shoulders.

"Are you going away?" Kenny asked, pointing to the suitcase.

"Yes," Mrs. Von Desch answered, "and some beople should be happy." Her accent was thick. She looked very hurt. "Boking their noses in other beople's business!" She looked across their heads, then turned away, dismissing them.

Had Oscar told his wife about her and Buddy? Leslie wondered. Could Mrs. Von Desch realize they were responsible for the police going to Overton Steel Company? Now her guilt came flooding back. She wished she could talk to Buddy about it. But it wasn't his fault that Mrs. Von Desch had been hurt. She was the one who had called the police.

By the time school let out, she had pushed Mrs. Von Desch to the back of her mind. She wanted to find Kenny, get home in a hurry, and then go to see the flag.

When they arrived at the tower, she looked up. "It's

really finished," she said. It was glorious. She wanted to dance up and down the old tar road in front of the farmhouse. "It's great," she said, over and over.

"Yeah, neat," Kenny agreed. "But what's that burlap bag nailed up there for?" It covered something near the bottom corner of the flag. The ladder up to the platform was still there, too.

"That's a secret—until Mr. Zimmerman gets here." She looked around and saw Dave packing things into his truck. He came over to them with a wide grin.

"It sure is great," she said again.

"Yeah, neat," Kenny repeated.

Dave nodded. "Glad you like it." He glanced toward the house. "Here they come now." Mr. Zimmerman and Leonard were walking toward the tower. "Now we can have the unveiling," Dave added. "I told them it was something special and they had to wait till you got here."

Dave went to the ladder and climbed up. Then he called down to them, "All of you, just stand there."

Leslie held her breath. Would it be as she'd pictured it? Dave undid the burlap bag and let it drop. There, on a slender gold line drawn from the corner of the flag, dangled a single gold star in honor of one who had died for his country.

"Oh, it's beautiful," Leslie said. She turned to Mr. Zimmerman. "That's Walter's star."

Kenny was jumping up and down. "Boy, that was a good secret."

Mr. Zimmerman's face crumpled and tears ran through the wrinkles down his cheeks. He hung his head and his shoulders shook.

Leslie, upset, didn't know exactly what to do. She put her arms around him clumsily. "Don't cry. Please don't cry." Tears filled her own eyes as she tried to swallow away the choking feeling in her throat.

The war was different to Leslie now. This was the nearest she had come to seeing it tear someone's heart out.

By now Dave had climbed down, and he silently laid his hand on Mr. Zimmerman's shoulder. Kenny, who had been looking bewildered, suddenly said, "It sure is a neat flag."

Mr. Zimmerman lifted his head and looked up at the tower a long moment. Then he sniffed and tried to smile. "It sure is."

Leonard had been standing by, rubbing his hands up and down the sides of his overalls. "Yes, it is," he said. "Thank you all so much." He looked at his father. "You okay now, Dad?"

"Yes, I'm okay."

Leslie had herself in control again. "Thank you very much for letting us use the tower and helping and—and everything."

Mr. Zimmerman nodded and patted her shoulder. Then he and Leonard turned toward the house. Leslie stepped quickly after them. "And thank you for not telling on us about the trouble we caused the other day." Mr. Zimmerman looked puzzled for a moment. "When Kenny and I tried to help paint the flag," Leslie explained.

Mr. Zimmerman's face brightened and he managed a little grin. "It's forgotten." He patted her shoulder again.

Dave was taking the ladder to the barn. Kenny followed him, and Leslie ran after, thinking, Now I have to ask him about the cost of the paint. He might have needed more.

"Do we owe you anything for the paint?" Her words were quick.

"Nope," Dave answered. "We needed only a tiny bit more. I went to our supply company for it. Let it be my contribution."

"Oh, thank you." Leslie sighed in relief.

"You owe me only one thing," Dave added. "A cup of coffee with your father. I'll enjoy some navy talk."

"Yeah, sure," Kenny put in. Dave touseled his hair, grinning. Then he turned back to Leslie.

"Oh, and another thing—a man from the newspaper came by this afternoon with a camera. I told him no—this is a secret—and that I'd let him know when to come back."

"Good." Leslie certainly didn't want it in any newspaper at all until after Papa saw the flag.

"And the red paint you bought," Dave said, "was a little darker." He pointed. "The strokes you made look like shadows and fit in fine."

Leslie squinted at the flag. Knowing where she'd painted, she could see the slight darkening in the red stripe. Her strokes were there. She had helped paint the flag!

"Yes," she told Dave. "I can see them."

"And I can see mine," Kenny put in.

Then Leslie asked Dave about something that had been puzzling her. "You said a friend of yours was going to help. We never saw him."

"Yes, he was here just once. You didn't come around that day. He painted the blue field for the stars. He had some blue paint at home."

"Please tell him we thank him, too," Leslie said, and then added, "We're sorry we caused so much trouble the other day."

"Think nothing of it," Dave told her. "See you kids later." He headed toward his truck.

Leslie looked back at the flag. Everything concerning it had turned out fine.

Now that the flag was finished, Leslie wanted to shout the news to everyone, but Papa had to see it first. She didn't know how she'd wait for him to get home and then even longer to tell Miss Ellinger on Monday. She hoped Miss Ellinger would have all the kids go to see it.

At least Saturday was a busy day with no time to mope. During the morning, she did her chores. Then she remembered that Mama was going to Benjamin's right from work. Leslie intended to be there early. If Mama missed the trolley car or it was late, she might not get to the store in time. And this was her last chance to get new stockings before Papa came home.

The more she thought about it, the more Leslie knew that Mama might need some help. She had gotten the big flag for Papa—she grew warm inside just thinking about it—now she must make sure Mama got what she wanted.

At twelve o'clock, she told Kenny, "Get ready to go downtown. We have to help Mama."

"I'm not going to stand in line again," Kenny said.

"You won't have to. Now come on."

Twenty minutes later, they hurried into the store. On the way to the hosiery department, Kenny complained, "I wish Mama would paint her legs. I'm tired of going for stockings."

Leslie ignored him, but when she stepped into line,

•

she whispered to him, "Go outside and wait for the trolley. When Mama gets off, tell her to hurry. I'm saving a place for her."

As the line moved, Leslie grew worried. The sales-lady was the same one who had told her to leave two weeks ago. Mama's note was in her pocket, but would it work? She wished Mama would arrive. Finally she was near the counter, with just two ladies ahead of her. She kept craning her neck toward the door. The woman in front of her was being waited on when at last Kenny burst in, pulling Mama by the hand. Mama stepped into line just as it became Leslie's turn.

"Sun beige, please, size nine," Mama said, out of breath. The hosiery was rayon, but so what, Mama was getting new stockings.

"Well, of all the nerve!"

Leslie heard the angry voice behind her and her face grew red. When Mama took her package, another woman said, "Why don't you wait your turn?"

"It was her turn," Leslie said quickly. "I saved it for her."

Mama added, "I'm sorry, but you're no farther back in line than you were before."

Outside, Mama pressed her package to her. All the way home, she held it like a bag of gold. Getting the stockings had been a pain in the neck, Leslie thought, but worth it.

After a late lunch and a short rest, they all headed for the theater. Mama was scheduled to sell stamps and bonds before the 3:30 show. They would be allowed in free after the show started. The movie was one with plenty of women in it, nurses and prisoners of war in the South Pacific. Leslie liked that kind because she could pretend she was one of those brave women.

As she watched the people going in, Leslie saw a group of boys from her class. Buddy was with them. There ought to be a law against having to see school kids on Saturday, she thought.

The next moment Buddy came over to her. "Remember the other day?" he began.

Good gosh! Was he going to blab about their going to Von Desch's right there in the theater lobby? She got up quickly. Mama was making change for a man buying a war bond. Kenny was doodling on a scratch pad. Leslie stepped away from them.

"Over here," she told Buddy.

"I just wanted to ask if you thought yet about reporting Von Desch?" Buddy asked.

"Yes, I thought about it. Now good-bye." She was afraid to tell him she had already called the police. He might blurt out the whole story to someone.

He looked puzzled, but she left without another word and went back to Mama at the stand.

It was almost dark when the show ended. As they left the theater, Mama said, "We'll have to hurry and have supper and then get everything ready for Papa."

At that moment, the school kids pushed past them. Leslie caught a glimpse of Buddy. But she certainly didn't want to think about Buddy and Von Desch now. Papa would be home on the train at five o'clock the next morning.

"We got the lamb roast," Mama went on as they walked along. "I wish we could have gotten some of that new powdered coffee that Papa likes."

"Yeah," Kenny said, "but Tony's father said they put it in K rations. Maybe Papa will get some when he goes overseas."

"I guess you're right," Mama agreed. Leslie could see her wince at the word *overseas*.

They had almost reached the house when they all seemed to see it at once. A light was on in the living room. Mama stopped, catching Leslie's arm on one side and Kenny's on the other.

"We didn't leave the lamp on when we left, did we?" she whispered.

"No," Leslie whispered back. Robbers? She shivered.

Kenny shook his head, pulling on the peak of his baseball cap.

Then Leslie saw a form in the shadows on the

porch—a man. She stiffened. Mama must have seen him, too. Her grip tightened on Leslie's arm.

The form moved and stood up. "Well, it's about time you gallivanters came home."

Then Leslie saw the dark blue pea jacket over the navy uniform. It was Papa! In a moment, there was a flurry of hugs and kisses and questions. Finally they separated and calmed down.

"It was a last-minute thing," Papa explained. "I got out of camp earlier than I expected and managed to catch the afternoon train. This is much better than getting in at five tomorrow morning." He gave them all another hug, then made believe he was pouting. "But I had to sit here and wait till you came back from the theater."

"How did you know where we were?" Kenny asked.

"A heavyset boy passed by and told me."

Good old Buddy, Leslie guessed. She bristled when she thought of Buddy seeing Papa before she did.

They were scarcely inside when someone knocked. It was Ruthie.

"Oh, Papa," she cried, "it *was* you. I thought I saw you when Mother and I drove by about twenty minutes ago, but Mother said you wouldn't be here till tomorrow. I took a chance and came over, anyway." Ruthie's eyes were shining. "I had to give you this. I knit it for you."

She held up—what else? Leslie thought—that dumb sweater.

Papa took the sweater, held it against himself, and laughed his quick laugh. "Ha, just what I needed. Thank you, Ruthie." He kissed her cheek. "Thank you very much."

Leslie had known Papa would fuss over the sweater, so she wasn't surprised. And Ruthie looked as if someone had just declared her queen over all the land.

"Sit down and have supper with us, Ruthie," Mama said.

"Oh, no, Mother's waiting for me. She was setting the table when I left. Besides, you all want this first evening to be just family."

Leslie was glad Ruthie had that much sense.

"We're going to Grandma's tomorrow," Papa said. "Why don't you come with us?"

Ruthie clasped her hands together. "Would it be all right?"

"Certainly," Papa answered. "Say hello to your mother for me. I'll see her soon."

Ruthie left. The evening sped by and Leslie was all ears as Papa answered their endless questions about the Seabees.

"Will you have to fight, Papa?" Kenny wanted to know.

Papa didn't say yes or no. "Well, Seabees are trained

for combat. If they have to fight, they know how, and they often do. Mostly they build roads and bridges so tanks and trucks can be brought in. And they put up buildings and air bases and take care of them." He ran his hand across his stiff dark hair. "Our motto is We Build, We Fight." He sighed. Then he laughed and touseled Kenny's hair. "But who knows, the war might be over before I get there."

"That would suit me fine," Mama said.

"Me, too," Leslie agreed.

"Will you pitch to me when you have time, Papa?" Kenny had switched to his favorite subject. "I practiced like mad."

"Sure thing," Papa promised.

12

Early Sunday morning, Leslie got up before anyone else and sneaked downstairs. It was still dark outside, but she took the flag from the hall closet. The air was nippy and her fingers fumbled as she fitted the pole into the holder on the porch post.

A short while later, Mama came down and started breakfast. Then she called Papa and Kenny.

"I peeked out the front window to see how the weather was," Papa said as he sat down at the table. "What's the flag out for?"

"For you, Papa," Leslie said. "In honor of you."

"Oh, thank you, thank you," Papa said, smiling quickly. "That's very nice of you—makes me feel like an admiral."

All through breakfast, between mouthfuls, Leslie and Kenny tried to help Papa catch up on the news.

"Our room lost the pennants for the paper and grease collections," Leslie told him, "but we did win the one for cans."

Papa grinned again. "Well, great. Hang out the flag!"

"We did," Kenny shouted, looking quickly at Leslie.

"In a big way," Leslie added. "But that's all we'll tell you for now." She gave Kenny a warning glance.

"The flag out front?" Papa looked puzzled. "It's the same one we always had."

"We know," Leslie said, still watching Kenny. She'd skin him if he gave away her surprise. She saw Mama give Kenny a warning look, too.

Then Mama told Papa she had two days off, Monday and Tuesday. She also told him about her new stockings and how she got them.

"Fine," Papa said. "Just in time, too. We'll be wanting to go out this week."

It was still quite early when they all left the house for church. As they got into the car, Mama gently took the baseball cap off Kenny's head.

"Aw, Mama." Kenny let out his usual groan.

Papa laughed. "Do you want the church roof to fall in? It will if some of the congregation ladies see that cap, even if you wear it only to the church door."

Every week there seemed to be more uniformed men in the pews, Leslie thought, glancing around. There was a prayer for the servicemen, as there had been every Sunday since the war began. It was a prayer asking God to bless our boys and bring them home safely, to establish peace and help us to forgive our enemies.

Leslie had trouble with the last part. She would try to forgive their enemies, but if they hurt Papa she didn't know how much success she'd have.

On the way home from church, Kenny asked, "Papa, will we win the war?"

Papa sighed before he answered. "I sure hope so, after all the lives that have been lost and countries torn apart. Yes, Kenny, I sure hope so. We must."

As soon as they reached home, they packed into the car everything they were taking to Grandma's house.

"We have to wait for Ruthie," Kenny said.

Not anxious to spend a whole day with Ruthie, Leslie said, "Maybe she's not coming." But no such luck. At the last minute, Ruthie came running down the street.

"Sorry to be late," she said breathlessly, and seated herself between Leslie and Kenny on the backseat.

Driving south through town, they came to the road that ran past Zimmerman's place. When they neared the farm, Leslie said, "Papa, stop in front of the water tower."

"Why?"

"We want you to see something."

Papa pulled up across the road from it.

"Look," Kenny shouted and pointed. "We had it painted."

Leslie felt a little annoyed by the word *we*. The painted flag was her idea. But she didn't say anything. After all, Kenny had told her about the billboard near Tony's place, and that was where they had met Dave.

Papa looked and stared openmouthed.

"It's to honor all the servicemen," Leslie told him, "but mostly it's for you, except for the small gold star. That's for Walter Zimmerman. He was killed in New Guinea."

Papa looked down at his hands on the steering wheel. "Oh, I'm so sorry. Poor Walter."

Leslie glanced at the small gold star. Please, she prayed, please don't let us ever need one for Papa.

Papa looked at the tower again. "It's a grand flag. Please thank everyone who worked on it."

"We did," Leslie told him. "And one man—his name is Dave—wants to meet you. He was in the navy, but he got wounded."

"Sure thing. I'll see him before I leave," Papa said.

Ruthie had just sat staring at the tower. Now she asked with wonder in her voice, "You had that painted, Leslie?"

Leslie felt smug. "Yes, I did."

"Oh, how wonderful. That's the greatest present

you could have given Papa." Ruthie squeezed Leslie's arm, "You're a terrific cousin."

Leslie didn't know what to say. When Ruthie was showing them the sweater she'd knit for Papa, Leslie had felt nasty and spiteful. Now Ruthie was genuinely happy and proud of Leslie's present to Papa. "Thanks," she managed to murmur.

Papa started the car and began to sing, "Oh, how I hate to get up in the morning." They all joined in and sang for several miles.

When they fell quiet for a few moments, Kenny asked, "Are you going overseas, Papa?"

"I'm afraid so, son. As soon as I get back to base."

Mama was silent, and Leslie wished Kenny wouldn't talk so much. But it was a glorious day. Some of the leaves were turning, the sun was warm, and more than once Leslie spotted a pheasant rising from the fields bordering the highway. Sometimes a rabbit or chipmunk hurried nervously out of the way of the car.

No one spoke for a while. In the quiet, Leslie thought again of the flag on the tower. Ruthie had given Papa a sweater and Kenny had practiced his pitching for Papa, but, to her, the flag was the best present of all. Of that she was sure.

Suddenly her thoughts switched to Von Desch. If she didn't have to think of what would come of her call to the police, she knew Papa's leave would be even happier for her.

When they reached Grandma's house, they found her waiting for them on the front porch—alone. Grandpa had died three years before. Grandma hugged Papa long and tightly. Leslie thought she would cry, but Grandma didn't. She tried to laugh. "Come in, come in," she said, and gently pushed each one through the doorway.

Mama gave her the basket. In it, besides the lamb roast, Leslie knew, there was some sugar and coffee. Mama wanted to be sure Grandma wouldn't run short of rationed things because of their visit.

Papa's brother came over from the next town with his wife and Leslie's two cousins. While the men smoked and talked and drank coffee, the women started to prepare dinner. Ruthie joined the women.

Kenny, already fidgety, suggested, "Let's play hide-and-seek."

Leslie was just as eager as he to go outdoors. So were their two cousins. They played and hid all around Grandma's yard and garage. Then they took a walk to a small park three blocks away and explored every inch of it until dinnertime.

And what a wonderful dinner it was.

"Here's hoping we will have many more times like this," Papa said, "even though we may have to wait a while." Then he told all about the tower flag. Leslie was glad he did—she didn't want to brag about it herself.

"Great, great," Papa's brother said, and Leslie's heart warmed with happiness.

"You really should see it," Ruthie put in. "I wouldn't have thought of that in a million years." Again, Leslie felt kinder toward Ruthie than she had ever thought possible.

Finally, when everyone exclaimed about how full they were, Grandma coughed lightly and stood up. "I think it's time for dessert." She brought in her golden carrot cake with almond-flavored icing. "Your favorite." She beamed at Papa. "The sugar I used couldn't be put to better use."

"Thank you, thank you." Papa shifted forward on his chair. "I know I'll do it justice."

As Grandma watched Papa enjoy the cake, her eyes filled with delight, then with sadness.

When at last it was time to leave, Leslie felt that Grandma's hug was tighter than ever before. She wondered if it was a lonely, frightened hug. Then Leslie said good-bye to all her other relatives and went with Kenny and Ruthie to the car. She knew Grandma would want to linger over her good-bye to Papa.

On the way home, Leslie noticed that the evening sky was bright with stars and a sliver of moon. She wondered if the sky was as pretty over war-torn countries.

With thoughts of the war came thoughts of Von Desch and his wife. Had he really done anything wrong? If he hadn't, would her call to the police hurt him or his wife? The same old guilt feelings came back. As usual, she tried to push them away. It was Papa's leave that she wanted to dwell on.

When they passed the water tower, Leslie craned her neck. Yes, she could see the flag even in the dark. But hard as she tried, she couldn't make out her red strokes. Still, she knew they were there.

Papa looked upward, too. Then he glanced over his shoulder. "That flag sure looks good up there," he said. "You couldn't have picked a better place for it."

Leslie nodded, feeling pride swell within her. She was glad Kenny was sleeping, so he couldn't butt in on her happy moment. Ruthie and Mama just nodded silently.

"And don't forget to give me Dave's phone number, Leslie," Papa added. "I'll call and see if we can get together."

"Okay."

Kenny was still asleep when they reached home. Ruthie started up the street immediately.

"Thanks a million. I better go right on home," she

said, walking backward. "Mother will be waiting." She gave them a little wave.

"Glad to have you," Papa told her.

Once inside the house, Kenny was wide-awake. He grabbed the comic sheets from the Sunday paper and gave half to Leslie. Before she looked at them, she went outside for the flag and put it in the hall closet.

"Well, we have four more days," Papa said as he and Mama settled on the sofa. Leslie saw Mama's eyes cloud. Four days were so few. "And," Papa went on, "we're not going to let the war keep us from enjoying them. With this fine weather, we could still have a picnic in the park."

"Great," Kenny said. "Let's get up early and pack a big, fat lunch."

Papa laughed. "You have to go to school, but we could go as soon as you get out." Then he added, "You said the key words—get up early. That means go to bed early."

Kenny groaned. Leslie did, too, inwardly. She wished she could stay up all night and talk to Papa about the Seabees. She would take notes, and if Miss Ellinger ever wanted another essay about servicemen, she'd be able to hand in a good one.

Rising, Mama piled the newspapers neatly and straightened the sofa cushions. "Come on, you two," she said. "Time for bed."

"Just a few more minutes," Leslie said, leafing through the comic sheets.

"Yeah, please," Kenny begged.

"You will go to bed now," Mama said.

"I didn't see all the funnies." Kenny kept on reading.

"Will you *please* go to bed," Papa ordered.

Slowly, Kenny folded the sheets. Leslie sighed and folded hers, too.

Going to the stairs, Kenny challenged her, "I'll race you up." His feet thumped on every step.

Leslie ignored him.

13

The next day, Leslie missed Mary on the way to school and ended up behind some boys. Buddy was hanging on to the group, trying to get their attention. "Hey, guys," he called, "know what?"

"No, what?" one said with a laugh.

"We heard from my Uncle Ben. He's in the merchant marines. They're not like the other servicemen." Buddy was talking nonstop. "You sign up for each trip, not like the navy, where you get orders to . . ."

The boys kept going. Buddy fell silent and slowed up. Leslie could see he felt snubbed, and she was sorry for him.

She asked, "Where does your uncle live?"

"Connecticut. We got a letter from my aunt yesterday and she said he's out on his first trip—on an oil tanker." Buddy grew talkative again. "Boy, that's dangerous. They get hit by a torpedo—one poof, and they're gone." He went on telling her about the merchant marines until they reached the school steps.

When the bell rang, Leslie was glad to break away from him. She hurried inside and put her things in her desk. Then, right away, she told Miss Ellinger that Papa had seen the flag.

"Good," Miss Ellinger said. "Now we can tell the class to go see it." As soon as class began, Miss Ellinger did so. "It was the suggestion in Leslie's essay about what to do for the servicemen, and it was finished just in time for her father's leave."

Buddy's hand shot upward. "I saw it yesterday. It's the biggest flag I ever saw."

For once Leslie appreciated Buddy's interruption.

At recess, he came up to her. "Gosh, that was a swell idea."

Then he leaned closer. "I still think we should report Von Desch."

Leslie would have liked to tell him that she had already called the police. It would be a relief to share it with someone. But Buddy was too blabby.

"Well," she said, "it does seem like he's doing something wrong, but what?"

Buddy shrugged. "I don't know, but maybe later we can find out something more," he said. Then he walked away.

The warm weather, ideal for their picnic, held through the day. Leslie and Kenny had never before walked home from school so fast. Mama and Papa were waiting with everything ready to take to the park. But the picnic would have to be a short one, since it was already after three.

Papa played pitch and catch with Kenny, and Kenny showed off his pitching skill to Papa. He hadn't had a chance to at Grandma's yesterday.

Mama and Leslie picked out one of the big wooden tables and spread it with a cloth and food.

They finished eating just as the sun was setting.

"We must get home now," Papa said. "Ruthie's mother is stopping by. I haven't seen her yet."

"This is just supper in the park," Kenny complained. "No games, no swimming, no nothing."

"Here, now," Papa said. "The most important part of a picnic is eating. And you sure did plenty of that." Then Papa looked dreamy. "Maybe the next one we'll have will be an all-day one, and we'll have a rip-roaring good time." Then he laughed his quick laugh and slapped Kenny on the back. "Now help gather up the things and stop grumbling."

Mama just smiled and touseled Kenny's hair. Leslie knew Mama was hoping the all-day picnic would come about soon.

The following day, Leslie again saw Buddy on the way to school. She and Mary were walking about a quarter block behind him. He was alone but didn't seem to be in a hurry to join the boys ahead of him.

When they reached school, Buddy looked around but still made no move to push his way into any group the way he usually did.

As Leslie and Mary came abreast of him, he looked at them and said, "My Uncle Ben is gone."

Leslie was puzzled. "I know. You told us yesterday. He's in the merchant marines."

"I mean he's dead." He stopped and spoke quietly. There was no bragging in his voice. Several of the boys stepped near to listen. "The tanker was torpedoed in the Atlantic. They'll never find any of the men. Just a big blaze, and it was over." Buddy looked straight ahead, his eyes unblinking. "I liked my Uncle Ben."

At last, Leslie thought, Buddy had something genuinely important to talk about, something the kids listened to, but it was something he couldn't enjoy or take glory in. She felt deeply sorry for him.

First Mr. Gillis's son, then Mr. Zimmerman's Walter, now Buddy's uncle. War was so rotten. She had no desire anymore to do something great for the war effort—it would be a million times better to do something to end the war.

When they went into class, one of the girls whispered Buddy's news to Miss Ellinger. Miss Ellinger went over to him and put her arm around his shoulder. "I'm so sorry, Buddy," she said. "Your uncle must have been a brave man to serve on a tanker."

"He was brave," Buddy agreed. "It was his first trip out. My aunt called my mother yesterday afternoon."

"Would you like to go home to be with your mother?" Miss Ellinger asked. "You could be excused."

"No, she said it's best that I come to school," Buddy answered. "She had a lot of things to do."

That day Leslie noticed Buddy didn't have to run after the boys. They waited for him and talked to him.

She and Kenny hurried home because Papa was going to take them all to a movie. When she told him and Mama about Buddy's uncle, Papa shook his head. "Those tankers—they carry hundreds and hundreds of gallons of oil. When they get hit, there isn't much chance of escape."

Mama was silent for a moment. Then she said, "Thank goodness you won't be on one of those."

Leslie thought of all the ships and planes that went down in the ocean. The ocean floor must be piled high with them. She wondered if the top of the pile would ever come up through the surface of the water.

Papa broke in on her thoughts by saying, "We have to hurry if we don't want to go in after the show starts."

They just had time to buy popcorn before the lights dimmed. The movie was a comedy—a war story about a soldier who did everything wrong.

On the way home, Papa said, "I forgot to tell you, Leslie, I called Dave today. We had a good chat, and we're going to meet for lunch tomorrow, since your Mama will be back at work."

"He's nice, isn't he?" Leslie said.

Papa nodded. "Fine fellow."

On Wednesday, Papa said he was going to take Mama out for the evening after work. The rest of the day, he said, belonged to Leslie and Kenny. After school, they just hiked around.

At the end of Laramie Street, Papa turned to go west. "Since Mama and I are going out for dinner," he said, "I'll get you guys a bunch of hot dogs in town. That little shop on First and Main has good ones." Then he teased them. "That is, if you two can hike that far."

Kenny hooted. "I could walk all the way across town."

At that moment, Leslie caught a glimpse through the gateway of Von Desch's place. There were boards nailed across the front door and windows.

Then Kenny stopped and shouted, "Look!" He pointed to the upstairs windows, which he could see above the high hedge. "They must have kicked Von Desch out."

Leslie told Papa about the talk that went around and about the police going to Mama's office.

"I guess there are lots of cases like that," Papa said.

"Do they always find the people guilty?" Leslie asked, then wished she hadn't. She didn't want to learn anything that would make her feel worse than she already did.

"Sometimes people haven't done anything wrong at all. They just look or act suspicious, and they're investigated."

Leslie felt worse than ever. She had trouble choking down one hot dog. "I'm not too hungry," she said, but she finished her soda.

"Well, now," Papa began, getting up from the skinny little table at which they'd eaten, "how about hiking down to the water tower to see the flag?"

Leslie thought that was a good idea. At least she would see something she had done right. When she looked up at the tower, she was filled with pride all over again.

While they were admiring it, Mr. Zimmerman came out of the house. Papa went toward him. "Hello, there," Papa said. "I want to thank you for letting Leslie have the flag painted on your tower."

"Glad to oblige," Mr. Zimmerman said.

"And I'm terribly sorry," Papa added, "about Walter."

Mr. Zimmerman nodded. Then, after a short chat, Papa said they had to leave.

On the way home, they passed a cardboard sign in a store window. It said SHHH. LOOSE LIPS SINK SHIPS.

Papa fell silent. Leslie glanced up at him. His face was sober and his stiff hair, ruffled by the wind, stood on end. He did not put his hand up to smooth it.

"You look worried, Papa."

"I guess I am. I might be thousands of miles away on the other side of the world. I worry about leaving your mother and you kids. Maybe I shouldn't have enlisted." He sighed deeply. "But I did and I'm proud to be in the service. Still . . ."

"Don't worry, Papa. Kenny and I will take care of Mama, and she'll take care of us."

"Sure," Kenny cut in, squaring his shoulders. "I'll take your place."

Papa, walking between them, squeezed them close. "I know you'll both do fine." He was silent for a moment. Then he grinned. "And I'm glad I enlisted. If I'd waited to be drafted, I'd probably have ended up in the infantry." He laughed and chanted, "Then I'd hike and hike and hike."

He was more cheerful now, but Leslie knew he was still worried. "I'll write often," she promised, "and let you know how things are going." And she would, no matter how much of a task letter writing was to her.

Then her thoughts drifted back to Von Desch. Maybe talking to Mama would help, Leslie thought, and she was glad to find Mama home when they returned.

"Mama, did you know Oscar Von Desch and his wife moved out?" she began. "We saw Mrs. Von Desch with a suitcase the other day, but now their house is all boarded up."

"Well, I don't wonder. I heard our company investigated him. I guess the pressure was too much for them." Mama paused. "The authorities may have been watching them for some time."

Leslie sincerely hoped so. Then she wouldn't be entirely to blame, no matter what happened. The next moment, she hoped Von Desch was a rotten Nazi. At least then she could be proud of turning him in.

If only she could tell Mama and Papa about calling the police. But Mama had warned her about meddling, and Papa was sure to say the war was bad enough without doing things to make it worse. She couldn't tell Mary, either. Mary would think her crazy for listening to anything Buddy had told her. At that point, she thought she'd even tell Ruthie if she got the chance.

Papa's leave was supposed to be such a happy time. She wished she had never listened to Buddy or been so anxious to do something important herself.

A thud on the front porch signaled the arrival of the paper. Kenny rushed out to get it. A moment later, he came back in with a loud whoop.

"Look!" he shouted. "The tower's in the paper." He held up a page. There, in the center, was a large picture of her flag. Mama and Papa exclaimed over it, and Leslie's spirits began to lift.

14

Thursday was an awful day for Leslie. She couldn't keep her mind on her work in class and was glad when the bell rang to go home.

Since Mama had to work, Papa announced that he was going to the Chinese restaurant to get their supper. "Tell Mama," he said at the door, "that she won't have to cook tonight." He swallowed his quick grin and left.

When Mama came in, she looked flustered. "I found out today," she said, "that the investigation turned up information on Oscar Von Desch and his accomplice—the man I saw him with on the trolley. I was shocked."

"Really?" Leslie held her breath.

"Will they kick him out of the country?" Kenny asked.

"I don't know what will happen, Kenny, but they were taken into custody over in Currey County this morning. That was fast. I wonder who informed on him."

"How about Mrs. Von Desch?" Leslie asked. She had to know.

"Both wives were taken, also," Mama answered. "Someone found out that they were in on it."

Finally, Leslie thought, she could breathe freely again. She wouldn't have to worry about innocent people being hurt. Now she could tell.

"Whoever called the police," Mama said, "did us all a favor."

"Mama," Leslie said, "*I* called the police."

"You?" Mama looked as though someone had given her a hard slap.

"I called and reported Von Desch."

Mama still stared at her. "I thought I told you not to meddle in anything like that. What if he were innocent and people looked down on him because of the questioning?"

"Well, I could tell he was doing something wrong when Buddy and I . . ." She stopped. She'd better not tell yet about sneaking around Von Desch's place, or about being caught by him.

"Yes? When you and Buddy what?" Mama prompted her.

"When we—when we were talking about it after

Buddy said Von Desch was a Nazi." Whew! She didn't lie, but . . .

Mama said no more. She just shook her head in disbelief.

Well, Leslie thought, the Von Desches would be getting what they deserved. Now that it was over, she should be pleased with herself for setting the law on them. But she made up her mind—no more spying or getting involved with the police.

She was so relieved that she helped Kenny drag out all the games to play with Papa. Papa had said they would spend his last evening together at home.

"This is first," Kenny said, holding up Parcheesi.

"Papa likes checkers," Leslie told him.

Kenny shook his head. "Parcheesi."

"How about mah-jongg?"

"Parcheesi," Kenny insisted.

"Okay, okay, Parcheesi," Leslie finally agreed. She could enjoy any game tonight, she felt.

Then Kenny asked Mama, "What did Von Desch do?"

"His accomplice was working at the plant," Mama explained, "and he gave Von Desch classified information, and Von Desch sent it on to someone else, I guess." Mama paused. "At any rate, the authorities felt their arrest had stopped a dangerous threat."

When Papa came in with a lot of little paper buckets of Chinese food, Mama told him about Von Desch. Papa shook his head in disbelief, just as she had done. Then Mama added, "I guess Leslie should get the credit for catching them."

Papa's eyes widened. "Leslie!"

Leslie didn't look at anyone.

"Yeah," Kenny told Papa. "She called the police." Then Kenny seemed more interested in snitching a bean sprout from one of the containers.

Papa laughed his quick laugh and just looked at her. "So our Leslie fired a shot for the war effort. Well, it turned out fine, but"—his face sobered—"you must be careful. Wartime is bad enough. Don't borrow trouble."

"Papa's right," Mama said. "You will do no more meddling." She dished out the chop suey before adding, "The whole story will probably be in tomorrow's paper. I looked and it isn't in this evening's."

"Probably," Leslie said. And Buddy would see it. Then he'd tell everyone he had helped catch Von Desch. Good. She didn't care. Let him have the credit—the kids would listen to him now. Only she didn't want him telling anyone that she had gone with him to Von Desch's place. She wasn't sure Papa would like that, or Mama, either. She would tell them herself sometime. She didn't know when, but it would be she who would tell them. She had to get hold of Buddy before school tomorrow and remind him. He might have forgotten that she had told him to leave her out of it if he decided to tell their secret.

"Don't either of you," Mama was saying, "talk too much about it. We've been cautioned about that—some people might get panicky and turn in innocent folks."

Leslie didn't need any such warning. She had had enough of investigations, police, and worry to last the rest of her life. She was tired of secrets. She'd feel free when she could tell Mama everything.

"Mama," Kenny began as he set out the Parcheesi board after supper, "why would spies want to go where you work?"

"Well, Overton Steel fills orders every day for the army and navy," Mama said. "We make parts for planes and ships."

Leslie remembered the little *E* (for *efficiency*) pin Mama got one day. She said everybody in the office received one—sort of like a government citation for the company's work.

"See, Leslie," Kenny said, "you kept Von Desch from—from—"

"Sabotage," Leslie filled in for him. Sabotage at Overton Steel—she hated to think of how awful that would be.

They were all enjoying the Chinese food when Papa

suddenly asked Leslie, "Think you might want to be a reporter when you get out of school?"

"No." She could answer that quickly and easily.

"Why not?" Papa looked surprised. "Change your mind about being a great writer?"

"No again. I want to write stories and books, but not news." She sighed. "I just couldn't stand wondering if I'd hurt someone or someone's family."

Papa leaned his head to one side and studied her for a moment. "Fine thinking, Leslie." He reached over and pressed her hand. "I'm proud of you."

No words could have made Leslie happier. She thought of Ruthie. This is what Ruthie missed—having her own father say he was proud of her. No matter how close Ruthie became, Papa was not her real father.

Funny, but thinking of Ruthie didn't bother her the way it used to. She didn't mind at all that Ruthie was going along with them to the station to see Papa off. But she was glad Ruthie hadn't butted in on their last evening together.

Losing almost every game of Parcheesi, checkers, and mah-jongg to Papa or Kenny didn't daunt her. It was a wonderful time. But she could see the sad look come and go in Mama's eyes. She knew Mama was thinking of tomorrow, when Papa would leave.

All too soon, she heard Mama say, "You two will go to bed now," and Papa ordering, "Will you *please* go to bed?" It seemed as if things had never changed. But they had—a lot. The war had changed everything. And tomorrow Papa would be going back to it.

Maybe he would be sent overseas until it ended. When she thought of that, her call to the police didn't seem so great, even with the results it had brought. Collecting papers and cans and grease wasn't so great, either, but that was what she was supposed to do on the home front, and she'd go right on doing it.

She helped Kenny put the games away and headed for the stairs.

"See you kids in the morning," Papa called after them. But he would see them only to say good-bye.

Mama was going to drive them all to the station to see Papa off on the early train. Then she'd drive Leslie and Kenny home to wait for school before she and Ruthie took the trolley to work.

Papa's leave was over. Tomorrow he would be gone.

"Race you up," Kenny said. He rushed past her and thumped ahead of her on the stairs.

She was halfway up when Papa called, "Leslie, thanks again—for my flag." He had used the word *my*.

Ah, Papa knew that in her heart the flag was for him. Now it seemed more special than ever. No matter where he was sent, she was certain of one thing— Papa would never again say "Hang out the flag" without remembering the water tower.